A Kind of Death

A Short Story and Poetry Anthology

Anthology copyright © 2019 Uncommon Universes Press. All copyright remains with original authors, who are the sole copyright owners of their respective works and retain all rights.

All rights reserved. No part of this publication may be reproduced, distributed, or transmitted in any form or by any means, including photocopying, recording, or other electronic or mechanical methods, without the prior written permission of the publisher, except in the case of brief quotations embodied in critical reviews and certain other noncommercial uses permitted by copyright law. For permission requests, write to the publisher, subject line "Attention: Permissions Coordinator," at uncommonuniverses@gmail.com.

Uncommon Universes Press LLC
621 N. Mulberry St.
Berwick, PA 18603
www.uncommonuniverses.com

This is a work of fiction. Names, characters, businesses, places, events, and incidents are either the products of the author's imagination or used in a fictitious manner. Any resemblance to actual persons, living or dead, or actual events is purely coincidental.

Supervising editor: Janeen Ippolito
Additional editing by Bethany A. Jennings and Sophia Heotzler
Proofreading by Sophia Heotzler
eBook formatting by Sarah Delena White
Print book formatting by Julia Busko
Illustrations by Julia Busko

Cover Design by Rachel A. Marks

A Kind of Death

Sophia Heotzler

I stood there on the edge
Toeing the line
Deciding to go left or right

One way led to gently flowing streams
Green pastures
And bright sunlight

The other led to raging seas
Hilltops
And cool breezes

One led to one future
And the other would've been different

One of them had you in it
And the other did not

I chose one way
I'll admit it
I did
I chose
I can't blame you

But I'll be honest
Sometimes I look over my shoulder
And feel my heart fill
With salt

It spills out of my eyes
And piles onto my lap

I blink away, hoping to see clearer
But I still don't remember it quite right

You're like that reflection of sunlight off the water
The stone skipping before it sinks to the bottom of the stream
The sand slipping through my fingers

But somehow

You made it into the creases of my hands
No matter how many times I rinse
You're still there

Every time I reach to the bottom of my heart
You're still there

And I think to myself that maybe
Those grains of sand aren't what's left of you
Maybe those grains of sand are what's left of me

I think when I turned one way
The other half of me crumbled into sand
Hoping that you'd follow the trail behind me

Hoping that this crumbling
Wasn't a kind of death

Eshe

Rosalie Valentine

I still remember the moment I began, the day I sprang to life. The world was younger then, full of wilder magic. The dryads and their trees were saplings, and the stars still remembered the day the mountain had been pulled from the depths of the earth.

"Eshe," a voice called.

I came into being in a streambed, surrounded by a lush mountainside in the throes of a quick, reckless spring. All I felt was confusion—not the frightening sort that I would learn later, but a sweet, wild wonder. I blinked at the sky above, a vault of endless blue.

I was all water and clarity, the light of the sun reflecting off and through me, rainbows sprouting from my countless prisms.

I flowed to my feet, though I did not realize that I had been lying down or what it meant to stand up; movement came to me like growing comes to grass. I searched for the voice.

"Eshe, here."

I swung around, and there was the voice, perched as a dove in the low-hanging branches of willow. Immediately, fondness and recognition tugged at me like a current. I belonged to this voice, this dove.

"My heart, my friend!" I cried, my voice bubbling and washing out of me. Newborn as I was, I knew not what I did not know, only that to see this dove and hear his voice made me overflow. I also knew not what to do after a greeting.

But the dove knew. "Eshe," he sang to me. "You are water and spirit—a naiad, and the lady of the mountain stream. Come, I have much to show you."

Without thinking, I followed him.

He taught me much—how my stream ran down the slopes of the mountain, filled by the snow that melts in the spring. He taught me of the days and the seasons and the stars in all their magic and wisdom and the trees and the creatures of flesh and bone that lived in the forest of the mountain. Of owls, nightingales, deer, mice, crickets, and fireflies.

Down the mountain, he took me to see where my stream met a river, and he showed me the river lord, Innes. Innes's river is where I first saw fish and otters. Soon, the fish left the river to travel up my stream, wriggling and pressing against my current, their scales flashing in the brilliant light. Delighted, I laughed at them, a sound as sparkling and frothy as the most excited, rapid parts of my stream. The dove laughed with me.

Then the dove told me he would go. "I shall return next spring," he said to me. "But remember that autumn will come after summer, and many things will die before winter."

"Die?" I asked.

"And you shall die too. It is like a type of sleep."

"Oh." Here I laughed again, for I had seen the badger sleeping in his den and the young hedgehog napping under a tree. "Then I shall die!"

He nodded, his dark little eyes fixed on me. "Yes. Much must die in the winter for the spring to bring newness."

I nodded at this, unconcerned. "And you'll return in the spring."

"Yes, I will return in the spring for you."

"All right." I felt my first pang of sorrow. It would be a sad thing for the dove to be gone for so long, but at least I would be asleep for much of it.

"The dying in the autumn will be hard, Eshe, but you needn't be afraid."

"All right," I said again. I didn't understand why I *would* be afraid.

The dove sang me a farewell song in a language I didn't know, and it was so beautiful that I sank to my streambed, shedding tears for the first time, tears both wildly happy and deeply sad. Then the dove flew away.

It was a merry summer. I skipped through the trees with the dryads and danced across the surface of my stream with the dragonflies. I sang to the fish and admired how the sunlight danced off my crystal waters and fluttered along the underside of the trees' leaves.

But summer does not last forever. As the days grew shorter, I found myself retiring to my stream often, growing tired easily. One day I lay stretched across the rocky streambed, staring up at the trees when my gaze fixed on the leaves. Instead of the vital green I'd grown used to, the leaves were fading to yellow.

As I watched, a leaf fell from the trees and landed in my stream. I surged from the streambed, plucked the leaf out of the water, and twirled it this way and that between my watery fingers. Indeed, yellow tinted the green.

When I showed the faded leaf to the dryads that evening before we set about dancing, they said simply, "Autumn comes, and then winter with the long sleep."

"Oh." I nodded, my confusion clearing. "Death. The dove told me of it."

And summer faded yet more while autumn left foretastes of its coming everywhere.

I swam down my stream, noticing my fish were absent along the way. How strange. I flowed all the way down to the great river but pulled up short. My stream ended before it came to the river. Instead of flowing into Innes's waters, it seeped and trickled in shallow muddy channels, struggling to reach Innes's currents.

That's when confusion came upon me in an altogether frightening way. A fish lying in the mud caught my eye. He lay wide-eyed and unmoving. I reached down to put him back in the water—fish weren't supposed to be out of water. I'd seen them grow panicky and flop around frantically, so I'd always helped them back into the water where they belonged.

But as I lifted the fish, he didn't squirm in my hands. He didn't move at all. I started to feel much as the fish seem to be when they're out of water—panicky and frantic. I set him in the river and released him, but he listed to the side and floated on the surface.

"Eshe."

I whipped toward the river. Innes, the river lord, appeared, his long grassy hair pooling around his waist. "He's dead."

I blinked. "Then how can we wake him?"

Innes shook his head. "He's dead. He will not wake."

"B-but the dove said death is like a sleep."

Innes approached me slowly, his murky eyes unreadable. "For some death is like sleep. For most it is simply death. No more waking, no more living, only ending."

I recoiled with a startled splash.

"Eshe," Innes said gently.

But I couldn't stay to listen. Sending water droplets in an arc, I fled up my stream and covered my face with my hands. The dove said I would die. This very autumn. I would die. No more waking, only ending.

Clarity dropped like a stone into my stream. My stream, which was drying up. It would stop flowing altogether soon, and I would die. Already the fish had left me, sensing if they stayed in my fading waters they would die too.

I collapsed in the deepest part of my streambed and wept bitterly. Within hours, my tears soured my stream. The creatures of flesh and bone would sniff my waters and pull away, my stream sullied by my grief and fear and anger, made unfit by my coming death.

I grew weaker as the days continued to shorten. The leaves on the trees faded to red and orange and yellow and dropped when the wind came. One by one, the dryads retreated into their naked trees yawning and promising to see each other in the spring. The bears lumbered to caves, and the mice buried themselves under the forest turf. The color left the leaves blanketing the forest floor, and they turned brown, drying. The flowers wilted and withered.

And with them I dried up. I wasted away, my stream shrinking day by day. I could no longer leave my streambed, too spent to rise. My weariness did not come with the yawns and sleepy smiles of the dryads. Instead, my weariness came with my voice fading away to a trickle and shallow breaths that sent my watery frame shuddering. My glorious hair that once floated and rippled with currents all its own hung limp and faded until it was gone entirely.

Though I had no tears anymore, I wept. Frightened and alone. Unable to move. Knowing death was coming and thinking this didn't feel like sleep.

One cool afternoon, the fading sun dried up all my water. A fit seized me as I never knew could come upon a water creature.

A horrible coughing and retching came upon me—silent yet shearing my chest. Gasping for life that was just out of reach, gone like my stream, I lay there.

Utterly parched. Drying up.

Cracking open, cracking open, cracking open, weeping because the dove had promised death like sleep, and this was nothing like sleep.

With a soundless cry, I split open one last time, and I died.

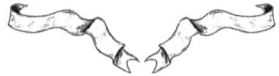

"Eshe."

I felt different somehow—deeper, wilder. I lifted my head and found myself on the bed of my stream.

"Eshe."

I blinked and lifted myself up, looking for the voice. There he was—the dove sitting beside my banks, my banks which were filled to the brim with freshly melted mountain snow.

"Spring has come!"

I looked around, my hair longer and fuller and more alive than I remembered, and I stared at him. "I died." My voice came out turbulent and rapid, confused and anguished.

"I told you that you would die, and I also told you that you would return in the spring."

"But it didn't feel like sleep. You said death was like sleep, but truly it is awful, like *ending*."

"It's not the end for you. You died, but now you are alive again. I told you of it, but you could not understand."

That quieted my rapids. But then he said something softly and gently, in the mournful coo of a dove. "And you will die yet again."

In response, I could only weep, sinking to my streambed. He flew off the bank and landed on the rock beside me, nuzzling my hair. "Eshe, these tears will make your water bitter as they did in the autumn."

At this, I could only weep harder, for I could hear the grief in his voice, could hear that I should not have made my water bitter for the creatures of flesh and bone, that I had made my stream something it wasn't supposed to be.

But then he sang to me, a sad song in that strange language, sad that I would die again. His sweet, sorrowing notes changed my tears until they were still distressed and confused but no longer bitter.

"Will I come back again in the spring?" I asked at last.

"Yes."

I nodded and rested my head on the rock where he perched. He cooed in my ear. "It is not an easy thing to die, but it is good to come alive again."

"I don't understand," I whispered, staring down the mountainside where my stream hopped and skipped.

"One day you will."

The dove stayed with me for an entire cycle of the moon. I told him of the last summer and dancing with the dragonflies. He told me of the world beyond Innes' river and where the fish go when they leave me and about the profound wisdom of the stars and how the dryads must sleep if their branches are to stretch further every year.

One day, I asked him, "Do other stream naiads die for the winter?"

"Some do. Many are fed by springs deep in the chest of the mountain."

My brow furrowed. "Why am *I* not fed by springs deep in the chest of the mountain?"

"Because you are filled by the snow on the heights of the mountain, the snow that sits in the light of the stars and melts in the spring to feed your stream. In the autumn, the mountain snow stops melting and freezes, and the water stops flowing to your stream."

I drooped. "But why may I not have a spring to feed me?"

The dove regarded me in a way that made me wish I'd kept silent—not angry or reproachful, just far wiser than I. "Because I desired you to be full of mountain snow."

This still seemed an insufficient reason, but I pretended to accept it, and when the dryads began to wake and emerge from their trees, the dove bade me farewell until next spring.

The dread of my coming death stilled me all through the summer. It was hard to dance with the dryads for they all fell asleep and didn't die every autumn. When I ventured down to the river, I discovered that Innes did not know sleep or death of any kind. At this, I almost made my stream bitter again, but I remembered how this had grieved the dove, so I held back my tears.

As autumn set in, I patrolled my stream, looking for any fish that may have gotten trapped in my death-destined waters as they flowed more shallowly. I found a school of minnows, and I shooed them down my stream until we came to the river. Already a muddy peninsula separated my waters from Innes's, so I scooped up the minnows one by one and deposited them into the river.

Innes came up out of his water while I was sending the last minnow on her way. "Preparing for winter, Eshe?"

I nodded. "I don't want any of them to get trapped and die."

"Will you return in the spring?"

I watched the minnows dart off down the river. "So says the dove." Before Innes could ask anything more, I left.

Death was harder that autumn.

While I wasn't so confused as I had been, knowing what would come seemed to make it more awful. The violent drying up overtook me as I lay there alone, dying. It seemed to take longer, to be more painful, more parching, more cracking.

At last, I died.

"Eshe."

The dove's voice called me back to life every spring, and every spring he stayed with me until the dryads began to wake.

Then one summer, after I'd died a dozen times, I discovered that the creatures of flesh and blood heard and understood my voice, and I understood theirs. There was a wildness and wonder in that summer akin to my first summer, all fresh and new and alive.

I could calm a frightened rabbit with the songs the dove first sang to me. I played hide and seek with the frogs, finding them in their muddy little burrows and laughing at their surprised chirps. The birds whistled and warbled to me about their babies—all wide-mouthed and demanding. And the fish listened when I told them that I was drying up and that they needed to return to the river.

When I told the dove of this the next spring, he sang to me and said, "If you had not died these dozen times, you would be like a spring-fed stream—unable to know the language of the beasts."

I collapsed into my stream, staring at him, heavy stones and bright rapids in my chest and no voice in my throat all at once. I managed to wash out, "How?"

"One day I will show you." And then he sang me a new song that deepened the awe filling my waters.

Dying grew more painful every autumn, lonelier, more parched, but I grew less afraid of it. Every spring and summer came with more profound sweetness, deeper and fuller as it seemed I grew deeper and fuller every time the dove called me to life.

One midnight I found that I danced without resentment with the dryads who went to sleep so gently and peacefully. After talking with Innes for hours, who knew no rest in sleep or death, I felt compassion for him who lived every cold winter with no companions. It seemed each of us required something different for our natures to flourish. For Innes, it was steadfast survival through the worst winters alone. For the dryads, simply rest. For me, death.

And then came the death that cut deeper and longer than any other by a hundredfold.

It took days.

I lay immobile, trapped, cleaving.

One evening, it rained, supplying enough water to prolong my barely alive existence for another few days. I'd never been so parched for so long, and every time I cracked open and thought I would die at last, I cracked open seven more times.

In my delirious dying, I wondered if perhaps this death might kill me so thoroughly that I would never come alive again.

I rived open again and again, splitting, cracking, parching, fragmenting. Then I died.

"Eshe."

I had never come so alive, every drop of me humming and bubbling with light and life. I rose, kinetic like never before, that sense of deepness, of wildness, of joy running through me more acutely than I could begin to describe.

"Eshe, come."

I found the dove hovering above the water.

"Hurry." His voice held such urgency that I leapt to follow him, splashed through the trees after him. We came upon a doe and an unmoving fawn. Death hung in the air.

I surged toward the doe; she bled too much, her breathing coming shallow. I murmured to her in the language of the dove, and the dove landed beside me. "The labor came too soon. The fawn is too little, and the mother is fading fast." There was mourning in his song that rent tears out of me.

"I have brought you here to help them, Eshe."

"How?" I asked.

"Heal them with your waters."

I stared at him. "My heart, my friend, I know not how to heal!"

"You have been emptied and refilled many times. Call your waters over them."

I stared at him a moment longer then shut my eyes. "Come to me," I whispered. "Come." With every drop of me, I called to my stream. Commanded it to come to me. Pleaded with it to obey my voice.

It came. I opened my eyes and saw a strand of water wend through the trees, gliding across the forest floor, sparkling and full of light. It mounted into a wave and washed over me and the doe and the fawn and the dove.

And death vanished from that forest glade.

The doe's breathing deepened, and the fawn stirred on the ground beside her. The dove lifted up a song, but I sat with no words.

The dove nudged me. "Eshe, come. It is time for you to go up the mountain."

Dumbly, I followed him. We climbed the mountain, following the path of drips and waterfalls that ran down to fill my stream. At last we came to the top covered in bright snow melting in the warming spring sun.

"Do you know why it is good to be fed by mountain snow even though it means you must die?" The dove asked.

"No," I whispered.

"It is good because the snow is full of the light and language and magic of the stars that shine down so close to this mountaintop. By this language you have been filled again and again with new magic. That is why it is good to be fed by mountain snow even though it means you must die. Because without the dying and drying up, you would not have known new water, new life, new magic. By this new water, you have been taught the language of the beasts and now you have been filled with water to heal. You never died in vain, and should you die a thousand more times, it will only bring more magic to you."

I could not speak, could only sink to the snow, wonder weighing me down and stealing all my words away. For the first time, I truly understood and believed it was good that I had perished those many times. And for the first time, my spirit could call my future deaths good.

I looked to the dove. "My heart, my friend."

It has now been over a hundred deaths since the dove took me to the mountain. He was right when he told me that I would never meet death in vain, for I am certain that each drying up has been met with richer filling, deeper magic, lovelier wonder.

Death is not easier. I am simply wiser.

It is good for me that the dove should give me the gift to die every autumn and come to life every spring.

It is good for me that I am a stream fed by mountain snow.

Ikra's Stone

C.W. Briar

"The last smile anyone sees belongs to the Hamakoshu."

Everyone knew that saying. Ikra learned it as a little girl. Later, after Ikra accepted Doshuban's marriage offer under the kepo tree, and after they built a house together, she taught the saying to her son. She also sang the Lullaby of the White Mask as she rocked the baby to sleep.

Dark night, dark eyes, at the door.
Little baby wakes no more.
White mask, cold mask, hides a smile.
Hamakoshu, kiss the child.

They named the boy Sooshan, though Ikra called him her little Sooshu. On stormy nights, she would recite the Hamakoshu Poem, which began with the line, "The last smile anyone sees belongs to the Hamakoshu." By this, Sooshan learned to honor the Spirit of Sleep.

Doshuban was a mason, so he would often be gone for days at a time, building walls and houses in the valley. Their family lived outside the village, near the kepo tree that had witnessed their first kiss. Sooshan loved to play in its shade, and it was there that they buried the birds and mice that their cat killed. Even tiny corpses belonged to Hamakoshu, so Sooshan had to learn how to show them respect.

He held up the pebble that Ikra had placed in his palm. "What's this for, mama?"

She guided his hand to the hole where she had laid the blue-winged finch. Together they set the pebble on the bird's chest.

"It's so Hamakoshu knows we honor his law," she said. "The animal did not die by our hands, so it belongs to the Spirit of Sleep. We show him reverence so he will smile in our final hour. You do not want to be someone who goes to final sleep under a frown."

Sooshan crossed his arms and pouted as she spoke. She thought it was because she had helped him. "You can place the pebble yourself next time, but it's important I teach you the proper way first."

"No, mama, you don't understand me. Why does Hamakoshu want a pebble?"

"Oh." Chuckling, Ikra hugged the boy to her breast. "I did misunderstand you. The pebble goes on the chest so the soul is held in the body, then Hamakoshu comes to collect it. I don't know why it must be a stone, but some things of the spirits are mysteries. The important thing is that we have done what's right."

Sooshan slipped from her embrace and ran to the far side of the tree. He peeked out at her, giggling as she covered the bird with dirt. The giggles turned into delighted squeals when Ikra stood and gave chase. After she caught him, Sooshan begged to be lifted onto the tree.

The boy lay on the lowest branch, proud as a puma. Sunbeams sprinkled over his back as the oval leaves turned in the wind. Ikra figured Sooshan's mind had already moved on from the bird, but then he said, "I wish Hamakoshu never came. I like Balku better."

Balku was the Spirit of Life and the brother of Hamakoshu. Instead of eyes of shadow, his eyes were like the sun. Balku's season was spring, and it was he who created life in the womb from love. In fact, he had already planted the seed of new life in Ikra's belly. A second child.

She had never seen Balku, nor had anyone she knew. His eyes were suns, after all, and who could see anything when staring into the sun? Tradition claimed that Balku's power was in his unheard song, so people honored the spirit by singing to Balku on people's birth days. That was the difference between the spirits; people sang about Hamakoshu and his power, but they celebrated Balku by singing *to* him. *By song came life, so with song was life honored.*

Smiling, Ikra placed her hand to her stomach to catch the flutters coming from her littlest one. Sooshan was correct that Balku was responsible for joyful things, so it was understandable that the boy preferred him. However, he needed to be careful to not blaspheme.

"My little Sooshu, do not fear Hamakoshu. You are young, and you're a loving, respectful boy. The spirit will certainly smile over you on your last day, but that will not come for many, many years."

But Ikra was only human, and humans cannot keep such promises.

Hamakoshu came for the boy in the winter, before his next birthday and before his next song to Balku. Hamakoshu's messengers, the three onyx crows, perched on the kepo tree that fateful morning. Their hideous cries awoke Ikra from Sooshan's bedside. She had fallen asleep after a long night of tending to her son. She recognized that nightmare sound. Anyone who had lost someone knew that sound. Death was imminent.

Her heart thundered like monsoon rain on the tile roof. She guessed that Hamakoshu was coming for her, or for Doshuban, or for their soon-to-be-born daughter. She had not thought it would be Sooshan even though he had suffered a cough for days. Perhaps she had not allowed herself to think it.

The boy's wheezing breaths would clear up. The crows would fly to another home, to torment a different mother with their strained, gargling caws. Ikra told herself these things as she put her son's feverish head on her lap.

When Hamakoshu's onyx cat appeared in Ikra's house, scaring away her own cat, it strode directly into the sleeping chamber. The feline was carved from black glass, and the thin tips of its tail and ears were hazy like smoke. In spite of this, the creature moved with as much grace as any living animal. It sat in front of the wood stove, unbothered by the heat, and stared at Sooshan's pale face. The cat's shadow stretched over Sooshan's chest, which rose and fell unevenly as he struggled to breathe.

With sinking heart, Ikra admitted what she had already known deep inside. When Hamakoshu arrived, he found her and Doshuban cradling the boy. They were struggling to sing a lullaby because of their sobs, and their song died entirely in the spirit's presence.

Hamakoshu was living darkness, a tattered flag of purest black. Every shadow was sucked out of nooks and corners and drawn into his body. Only light and white remained as the room turned into a sculpture of snow. Hamakoshu's mask was the same white color. The shape was feline but simpler, as though only the melted memory of what a cat looks like. The round eyes were empty, and the shadows in those holes were somehow darker than the spirit's body. The lower jaw of the mask had broken off, exposing Hamakoshu's red chin but not his lips.

The spirit glided to Sooshan with the ease of a bird carried by wind. He leaned over the boy's too-small body swaddled in blankets. An ethereal tendril stretched over his ribs, which shook from another violent cough.

Ikra was screaming Sooshan's name when the spirit's mask began to rise. She was supposed to avert her gaze, but she disobeyed. Was it curiosity that tempted her eyes to linger, or anger over one so young and innocent being stolen? Whichever the reason, she watched long enough to glimpse a smile on Hamakoshu's blood red lips. She was tempted to stare longer, to see more of his face, and to glimpse his true eyes. It would have been easy to let Hamakoshu take her soul as well, to leave this world with Sooshan.

But she looked away. She did so partly out of fear and respect, and partly because she doubted there would still be a smile if she stole a glance.

Sooshan was gone.

Ikra and her husband suffered their grief during the coming weeks. They hung ringed chimes on the kepo tree. Sooshan could return with the wind to ring them, and Ikra, large with child, would cry both tears of joy and sadness. Doshuban did the same, though he was better at hiding it.

Their daughter was born while Sooshan's death still reverberated. Within two years, Balku blessed Ikra with another daughter. Doshuban expanded their house, a new loft with a raised ceiling. The girls laughed together on the loft, drew pictures on shared pieces of slate, and slept up there on warm summer nights. The kepo tree continued to grow, raising its branches until only Doshuban could help the children reach them. Eventually, even he was not tall enough to lift them onto the boughs. Good moments blossomed from the brokenness like dandelions growing from cracked stones.

However, the blessings were only gaps between tears. The wound from Sooshan's death never fully mended. The boy's absence lived among them, sitting hungrily at their supper table, frowning while the rest of their family laughed.

Doshuban recognized Ikra's hurt, so he crafted a gift by which she could cherish the shortened years with their son. As always, their family sang to Balku on Sooshan's birthday. Afterwards, Doshuban presented her with a heart-shaped vessel of polished gray stone. Sooshan's name was etched into the lid. The inside of the box was lined with cloth from Sooshan's baby clothes, the shirts that Ikra could not bear to put on Sooshan's younger siblings.

How the gift warmed her cold heart! On windy days, Ikra and her girls carried it to the kepo tree. There they waited for Sooshan to ring the chimes, which sounded like metallic giggles. The girls would giggle themselves as they shut the box's lid, catching the sound of their brother.

Ikra loved the girls, but she only had the two, and she never had another son. She blamed herself for this. Had Hamakoshu punished her for her disrespectful glance at his face? Perhaps. Nevertheless, she did what she could to cherish the years with her daughters before life took them away like autumn leaves. The girls grew into women and grew apart, taking up residence with husbands from the valley. They birthed children of their own, and when they visited Ikra and Doshuban, there was laughter and singing anew. She taught her grandchildren to honor the spirits, and she chased them, giggling, around the kepo tree in spite of her creaking bones.

Eventually, one of the girls left for a distant village as she and her husband sought work. Then came the threat of war on the kingdom's border. That chased away their other daughter's family. The giggles of children stopped for a time, replaced by rumors of invasion.

War indeed did come. Ikra's and Doshuban's home was spared, but the village and its people were ravaged. Screams and clashes rose from the valley. Flames illuminated the hills. Hamakoshu labored long into the night. In the morning, there was only silence, smoke, and the waft of gore on winds that failed to ring the chimes.

Thus began the decline of Ikra's years. Doshuban had much work to do in rebuilding ruined homes, and that kept him away for many, many hours. Their dearest friends had perished or been chased off by the fight, their houses now inhabited by soldiers who spoke an unfamiliar language. Those were quiet years. Ikra's home ached for human conversation as she labored in and around it.

Her daughters still lived, but their visits became rare, separated by great chasms of time. The only childish giggles regularly heard under the kepo tree were those from the ringed chimes. No grandchildren's eyes widened with wonder as Ikra recited old stories. No one to hear the Lullaby of the White Mask, so she refrained from reciting it. Even the last of Ikra's cats disappeared. After its death, she buried it under the old tree, a pebble placed atop its chest.

At least she still had Doshuban, who was no small blessing. Had she not hoped for this when she first accepted his proposal long ago? Their lives had begun to wane, and still they had each other. On summer days, they would sit under the shade of their kepo tree, wrinkled fingers entwined, weary heads leaning together. He was still the man who delighted her with sweet whispers and unexpected kisses. They would open the stone box with Sooshan's name and pretend to hear the old captured bell chimes.

Through seasons of Balku's plenty and Hamakoshu's reaping, Doshuban had remained by her side. They had never lost their power to make one another smile.

Then one day the crows returned, poisoning the morning's peace with their hideous caws.

Ikra had forgotten many things but not the fear of losing Sooshan. One did not forget how grief could freeze and shatter a heart, or how the icy shards tear veins as they course through one's body. She and Doshuban looked up from their bowls of porridge. Terror lifted her from the chair and shoved her to the window.

Three crows were perched on the kepo tree. Sunlight glinted

off their onyx bodies and showed through the smoky tips of their feathers. Their eyes could not be distinguished from their equally black heads, but Ikra could feel their gaze boring through the walls of her home.

Their beaks opened in unison, and their raucous snarls caused Ikra to collapse to the floor. Doshuban had to help her to a chair. Ikra's chest throbbed. She assumed Hamakoshu was coming for her, yet when the spirit's black cat appeared atop their table, its gaze was fixed upon her husband.

Now it was Doshuban's turn to collapse from fear. He grabbed his hip after the fall, and his words were slurred by the purple swelling on his head. He groaned and muttered until the ache, becoming too great, put him to sleep.

This was how Ikra would enter into a life of absolute loneliness, watching her love's breaths dwindle to nothing. It was unlike Sooshan's rumbling, violent gasps for air, but the loss was too familiar. Bandages were unfurled from an unseen wound that had never healed.

Her soul rooted itself in her defiance and anger. She could not endure the torment of loss again.

Ikra would not wait for Hamakoshu's arrival this time.

She tucked wine-soaked hesipa leaves into Doshuban's cheeks. That would lessen his pain and keep him in sleep's care. She also placed a cool, damp cloth on his forehead and draped a blanket over his feet. As she did, her gaze stuck to the heart-shape vessel upon her shelf. Doshuban's gift had given her peace and joy, and now it gave her a plan.

Hamakoshu liked stones, no?

Ikra was holding the box when the spirit ascended the hill. Hamakoshu was a rag of night beneath the morning sun. When he glided up the road, he discovered Ikra waiting at the door for him. She would not cry this time. The spirit had stolen enough of her tears. Instead, she spread her feet to bar his entrance even though she knew Hamakoshu could pass through her walls as easily as through an open door. She hugged the stone vessel to her chest.

Hamakoshu drew closer, undeterred. What now? Ikra had no plan, and she was shaking with fear. One did not barter or make demands of Hamakoshu. He might raise his mask at her for such defiance. Was her first peek at his face, on the day Sooshan died, responsible for the losses she had suffered through life? How much worse would Hamakoshu's wrath be if she outright defied him? Would he smile on her when she died?

Insolence could cost her everything. A frown would mean never seeing Sooshan again, and that was her greatest fear. This life had given them so little time together. She did not want to sacrifice their next life as well, but she had to protect what she had with Doshuban. He was her first and oldest love.

Hamakoshu's shadow eyes saw through her to his goal. She was incorporeal to him, her soul not yet ripe for reaping. How could she, a mortal, command his attention?

Balku's name appeared in her frightened mind like a kind stranger in a time of need. Balku, whose eyes shone with golden light. Balku, whose name was praised with songs in joyful times.

Ikra's lips parted. Her tongue awoke. She sang. There was no strategy behind her song, no understanding of her compulsion, but still she sang. The Lullaby of the White Mask bled out of her mouth, and for the first time the words were not about Hamakoshu, but instead offered to him as if he were Balku.

Dark night, dark eyes, at the door.
Little baby wakes no more.
White mask, cold mask, hides a smile.
Hamakoshu, kiss the child.

Hamakoshu stopped. His white mask and red chin hung close enough to be touched, not that she would dare do such a thing. The frayed edges of his shadow writhed around her shoulders, and though her skin felt nothing, her soul sensed the chilling touch of his presence.

Ikra sang the song again, and then a third time. Hamakoshu drifted backwards. The holes in his mask now saw her, of that she was certain even if she did not understand her own certainty. She had the audience of death itself. Ikra had kicked the foundation of life, and the foundation shook.

In that moment, there was only Hamakoshu, Ikra, and the man she loved.

Ikra bowed her head.

"Eternal Hamakoshu, Spirit of Sleep, the keeper who stands at the border of the hereafter. I bear no claim over souls that belong to you, and yet I am ruined by loss. You have claimed so much from me, and I have only one I can lean on. Now you come for him as well. I beg you to reconsider or take us together. Do not leave me—"

Her eyes rained. The rivers of tears overflowed their banks. Ikra's sobs stole her voice, but she needed to finish her prayer. She could not expect this busy spirit to wait for her.

Ikra opened her eyes but did not raise them. She stared at the lowest tatters of Hamakoshu's form. He terrified her, and that fear steadied her.

"I beg you, Hamakoshu, do not leave me alone. Let Doshuban live a little while longer. Our days are short. What is a small wait to one such as yourself, who has existed from the beginning of time? To us ... to me ... every new day with my husband will be a treasure immeasurable."

Ikra raised her eyes until the mask was at the edge of her sight. The white shape hovered motionless, judging her. Ikra grimaced, waiting for the mask to rise and for a red scowl to drag her into eternal woe.

Instead, the pale feline shape moved to go around her. Hamakoshu was entering her walls when she stopped him with a shout.

"Halt!" The air crackled with an energy she could not describe. "I know I cannot claim Doshuban from you, but I am willing to trade. You are here for a life. Take some of mine instead. Give me but a little while longer, if you are willing."

Ikra held out the stone box. She heard a little boy asking why Hamakoshu wanted stones, and she still did not know the answer to that question, but the offering seemed right.

Her eyes were now level with the shadows in Hamakoshu's mask. The darkness deafened her and drained all color from her eyes.

The white mask rose ever so slightly, revealing a smile and nothing more.

Hamakoshu's form stretched over the box. Ikra felt her pulse migrate from her chest, first to her arms, then to her hands, and finally her palms. The box moved in a steady rhythm. Her heartbeat was inside of it. As for her breast, it became cold, rigid, and heavy as stone. Her fear and grief were muted, but so too were her happiness and joy. Ikra became a statue of herself.

Hamakoshu dragged the box out of Ikra's hands, then withdrew toward the kepo tree. The air circled around him, sending the chimes into a noisy, frenzied dance. Part of the spirit's body twisted into an arrowhead that pointed toward one of the tree's branches. A leaf dropped from the branch and swirled on the unnatural wind into Ikra's hands. Hamakoshu then sank into the earth, the place where Ikra had buried her son long ago. The heart-shaped vessel vanished with him.

Ikra opened her hands and looked at the leaf. It turned brown, grew crisp, and crumbled within seconds. She brushed the fragments off her palms. What did it mean?

She then walked into her house. The old Ikra would have run, hurrying to confirm her husband still lived, but this new Ikra with a stone chest felt no haste. She felt little at all. Her passion for Doshuban's life was no more than an itch that had to be scratched. When she found he still breathed, she was surprised she did not feel more relief, and she was surprised her smile could be so small.

Ikra came to understand the leaf over the following weeks. More of them fell, one-by-one, and they always crumbled to dust. As the branches became bare, they darkened. A few of them fell to the ground. The kepo tree, the symbol of her marriage, was dying. Hamakoshu had found one more thing to take from her. It ought to have crushed her, but her heart was too numb and her grief was running dry.

When the tree died, Hamakoshu would return.

Doshuban was never the same after his fall. He struggled to walk because of his hip, and his dependence on hesipa leaves meant he slept through much of each day. His mind was confused, his words thick molasses that came slowly off his tongue, but he was alive. His embrace was still as warm as ever.

As for Ikra, she now lived in a world of less flavor, less music, and less passion. There were stirrings and memories of love, especially when she cared for Doshuban or lay in his arms, but the love was dim. What had been a warm fire was now flickering candlelight. Nonetheless, it was the only light she had, and she was thankful for it. She and Doshuban shared the tiniest ember of joy to its fullest. Every moment was cherished without concern for the falling leaves glancing off their door.

Nothing was as it had been, but life was still beautiful, and Ikra still had cause to thank Balku. In spite of all that was wrong, she and Doshuban shared one of their finest years together. Every minute of life was a gold coin to be counted.

She knew when the last leaf fell because the tree groaned and toppled with it. The crash drew her outside. The ringed chimes lay useless and silent in the soil. The once-beautiful bark of the kepo tree was wrinkled, dark, and infested with moss. Few of the skeleton branches remained, and on one of them sat three onyx crows.

Doshuban was inside the house, deep into a hesipa-induced sleep. Ikra let him rest. Instead, she waited at the door for Hamakoshu as she had before. There was no emotion for what was about to occur, only knowledge of what should be done. She bowed in respect to Hamakoshu, then led him inside. This time the spirit's visit felt like the closing of a door rather than the entrance of a thief.

Doshuban lay in bed. His final breaths lifted specks of floating dust toward the ceiling. Ikra sat beside him. She placed his right hand, once the calloused and powerful tool of a mason, onto her lap. Hamakoshu drifted over the kindest man Ikra had ever known. The mask was raised, the smile shown, and color vanished from the room. Ikra closed her dry eyes.

Her husband's hand went limp. Hamakoshu had claimed what was his.

By the time Ikra finished digging Doshuban's grave, her hands were raw and blistered. Her clothes were dirt and sweat. A stone was placed on Doshuban's chest, for no reason other than tradition. Hamakoshu already possessed his soul.

Finally, once Ikra had finished burying Doshuban's body, she sat on the mossy husk of the kepo tree. There she waited, watching the sun set. Waiting, but waiting for what? She was alone, utterly alone, with only the chirping of crickets to fill the silence.

Ikra's many emotions threaded together as never before. After years of being tangled in a knot, her fear, sadness, and joy were now tied together in a bow. She felt no rush to return to her bed or eat. She would wait upon the tree and watch the moon sail across the darkening sea above.

A hand touched her back, or rather a form shaped like a hand. Ikra turned and faced something that defied understanding. Hamakoshu hovered beside her, staring toward the same moon. Not hovering over her, nor hovering in front of her. No crows had warned of his coming. He simply hung there as though sitting on the log with Ikra.

She started to get up, to hurry away from impending death, but her muscles were too fatigued. She simply relented, awaiting her fate. It was not as though she could escape. However, Hamakoshu continued to linger like an old friend. His form wrapped over her shoulders like a blanket, and though it gave no warmth to her body, her soul relaxed.

Her heart, though numb, felt comforted. Her mind failed to explain the sensation. She had known a lifetime of fear and deference to this spirit, and now that everything she loved was dead or gone, she suddenly wanted to be beside Hamakoshu. She had no desire to flee, to ask him to leave, or to cower. Instead, she welcomed this hated stranger's presence.

Perhaps this was the trickery of the spirit. Perhaps he came as a comforter to those he was about to kill. Ikra's suspicion seemed to be confirmed when the white mask rose. There was no reason to look away now. This was her end.

Or was it? Hamakoshu was not smiling, which terrified her. Was he angered by her bargain, or by her slow submission during Sooshan's death? She was broken by the thought of never seeing her family again. However, she realized Hamakoshu was not frowning either. He seemed sad. There was a sense of understanding on his part.

Ikra, struggling for understanding, was left with only confusion. Was that strange, though? Had she not taught her children that the ways of the spirits were mysteries?

The mask climbed higher, and golden light shone from eyes that had been darkest shadow. Hamakoshu's red face turned bronze in the glow, and colors rippled through his body. The area around him was bright as day even though the sun had been replaced by the moon.

Crickets, confused by the sudden change, fell silent. Their song was replaced by another, one with the gentle thrum of a harp and the melodious whistle of birds. The music came from Hamakoshu, but not out of his body. Instead it seemed to surround the spirit as well as Ikra.

A song?

Her jaw, which had been clenched nervously, now gaped in wonder. "Balku?"

The spirit said nothing, nor did he nod. His golden eyes were motionless, steadily illuminating Ikra's face, yet they conveyed the spirit's answer. He was Balku. Of course he was Balku. Nothing else could produce such an incredible song.

"Balku, you and Hamakoshu are one?"

Again his radiant eyes affirmed her question.

None of the lullabies, poems, or stories spoke of this. Ikra was being shown a grand secret, perhaps the grandest secret of them all. She had so many questions yet no desire to ask them.

Balku's body opened, and out from the shadows and rainbows there emerged a gray stone. It was half of the heart-shaped vessel that Ikra had surrendered to him. The bottom and lid of the box had been split, as had Sooshan's name. It now appeared to read "Sooshu."

Balku placed it in Ikra's hands. She felt her pulse again, flowing up her arms rather than out from her chest. Her emotions, both the wonderful and the cruel, rushed into her. She was overwhelmed to the point of paralysis and tears. Had she ever contained such powerful feelings before? Had her grief and joy truly been so immense? It seemed impossible that they fit into her body.

Ikra's chest felt soft again, the numbness gone. Her arms regained their freedom to move, and she wiped away the tears blurring her vision.

"I don't understand, Spirit," she said.

Balku scooped up soil and placed it in the broken stone box, which now resembled a bowl. Then he snapped a piece of bark off the dead kepo tree and pushed it into the soil. Balku's light continued to shine, and Ikra watched in amazement as new life sprouted out of the dirt. A green shoot grew, and two leaves emerged and spread wide.

New life had formed in her hands within seconds. It felt like she was holding all of the wealth of all of the kings.

She still did not understand the mysterious spirit, but she understood something new, something she had known all along but never truly grasped. Hamakoshu and Balku were one. From loss, there came gain. There was life, but without death, how could there be new life?

Ikra had hated Hamakoshu because he took, but did not Balku take as well? Had he not taken away Ikra's daughters through circumstances of life? Meanwhile, if Balku was the same as Hamakoshu and Balku could take, did that mean Hamakoshu could give blessings?

That unrecognized truth had always been right before Ikra. Hamakoshu was not known as a devourer or a destroyer. He was the keeper at the gate, the one who stood at the border. If there was a border, there was something beyond that border.

She would not be crossing that border. Not yet. Not that day. Doshuban would not be sleeping beside her that night. Sooshan, her Sooshu, would not be coming back to her, and she needed to wait to go to him. Hamakoshu and Balku showed her this, but he did even more. He continued to sit beside her on the old kepo tree, comforting her, singing the most beautiful song a person could hear. Together, Ikra and Hamakoshu watched the moon's glorious journey to the western horizon.

How deep the mysteries of the spirits.

Ikra leaned against Hamakoshu. She peeked only once in his direction. The spirit was smiling.

The Swan Women of Skye

Savannah Grace

All the best things were born and died in Skye, Scotland.

People outside of Skye didn't know that, but then, they had not been born in Skye, so how would they know? Only the people of Skye knew about the magic that imbued their skin and the stones beneath their feet, that roped through the low clouds hanging above their heads. The people of Skye were born into magic. Everyone knew. Mostly.

Lauren Dryletski didn't know.

Or perhaps she didn't not *know* so much as didn't *believe*.

She knew about Skye's magic—had felt it, even, burning beneath her brother's skin, and seen it in the sirens that swam just offshore. But never in herself.

Lauren Dryletski didn't believe that she was one of the magic things of Skye, Scotland.

"Rubbish," she would say, to anyone who tried to tell her otherwise. She knew better. No magic for her.

"Rubbish," she said right then, to the cashier at the tiny corner shop who'd call her pretty—though her lips did twitch into a cautious smile. Brown hair and a smattering of freckles might have been cute on a kid, but not an eighteen-year-old woman. She knew her place.

But it was nice to be appreciated.

The cashier shrugged at her response but smiled as well. "Suit yourself," he said, his fingers flickering softly blue as he put her purchase of boxed milk and day-old biscuits into a paper bag—the blue from his magic. Lauren wondered what it was, but she wouldn't pry. Not her place.

The cashier handed her the bag. "Have a good day, ma'am."

"Thanks," Lauren said, gingerly taking the bag before walking out of the corner store.

The cobblestones bled cold through the soles of her scuffed kitten-heeled shoes. Lauren pulled her cardigan close around her shoulders as she walked to her car. It was an old car, had probably seen as many years as God himself. Lauren didn't mind, though. The car was one of the few things her brother let her have, mostly so she could run errands.

She didn't get to have much.

Lauren settled into the scuffed driver's seat and plunked the paper bag onto the passenger side. Then she crossed her arms against herself, tucking her cardigan close, and stared at the steering wheel.

The car had been a convertible once, but the roof wouldn't cough up now. It would be a cold drive home.

Lauren sighed and grabbed the wheel between her chapped fingers. Nothing for it.

"Markus? I'm home …"

Lauren tip-toed over the slightly slanted threshold into the house, peering around the dim interior for her brother. "Markus?"

It was not, all things considered, one of the most run-down houses in Skye. There was a roof. Electricity still worked, though mostly only in the bathroom. The walls kept them from frostbite. What more could a person want?

But the house felt richer when Markus was gone. The days he was gone freed her to go out to the grassy cliff that rose above Skye and clear her head, take a breath, and spend time feeding the swans that frequented the pond there. She knew them all by name—she frequented that pond, too.

Giving a small huff, Lauren kicked off her shoes and walked into the kitchen. He wasn't home yet. He would have yelled out already.

Lauren put the paper bag on the table, then went to the cupboard to get a glass. A sharp cough broke the house's silence.

"I'm coming, Mom," Lauren said, hurrying to open the boxed milk and fill the cup mid-way.

Another cough, choking this time, answered her. Pursing her lips, Lauren carried the cup down the hallway to the house's single bedroom.

The door creaked when she opened it. Thin curtains covered the room's window, but shafts of pale Skye light filtered onto the frail, coughing figure in the bed that took up most of the room.

Quickly, Lauren sat in the upholstered chair next to her mother's bed. "Shh, Mom, shh …" She helped prop her up and handed her the cup of milk.

The woman's hands, made old at far-too-young an age, quivered as she held the cup and drank. Blue veins roped her skin like tiny rivers. She'd once had magic that made water respond to her touch. It had been lost when she got sick—*pity, pity,* the townsfolk had muttered when they heard.

To Lauren, it was more than a pity.

Lauren waited until the last drops of milk were gone, then eased her mother down and took the cup back, setting it on the floor.

"How you doing, Mom?" Lauren asked as she righted herself in her chair and pressed a smile to her face. The question was rhetorical. Her mother had only fallen deeper into illness since Lauren's father died ten years ago.

She hadn't spoken a word in three.

Lauren's mother smiled, wrinkles paving roads in her worn face. She reached out to pat Lauren's hand with her paper-thin one, and pointed to the window. Dust motes fluttered in the shafts of light. One of the curtains was torn, and they played around the frays.

Lauren shook her head. "Once you're healthy, Mom. Once you're healthy we'll leave together. I'm not—"

The front door slammed open. Both Lauren and her mother winced.

"Lauren?" a voice yelled. It was a coarse voice but young, one that spoke of cigarette butts littered on cobblestones and liquor bottles smashed on the sides of houses.

A knot coiled in Lauren's stomach. Gently, she stood and smoothed her mother's ratted comforter before planting a kiss on her forehead. "I'll see you soon, Mom."

Lauren quietly clicked the door shut behind her and allowed herself one deep breath before lifting her head and going back to the kitchen.

Markus had a face that made Skye girls swoon. Sharp cheekbones angled under glittering hazel eyes, and his wicked mouth curved into a smirk under a straight nose. All of the town agreed that Markus was one of Skye. He was too beautiful not to be. Maybe his beauty was his magic—Lauren had never bothered to ask.

But as she watched him angrily dig through the paper bag she'd left on the table, with the sunlight throwing shadows beneath his eyes, she wasn't so sure.

Crossing her arms, Lauren fiddled with the edge of her cardigan. "You need me?"

Markus snapped his gaze up to her face. "Yeah," he said slowly, his voice dangerous. He lifted the torn bag in her direction. "I would like to know what *this* is." A growl underlaid his words and there was a strange sheen to his eyes, still red from yesterday's hangover.

Lauren pressed her lips together. "Mom wasn't doing well, so I bought some—"

Markus slammed the bag back onto the table, making Lauren jump. He jabbed a finger at her from the other side of the room. "You were supposed to be getting yourself a job, not buying yourself a crapload of biscuits and boxed milk!" He smacked the bag onto the floor, and biscuits rolled across the cracked tile to bump into Lauren's feet.

To be more exact, two dollars and thirteen cents rolled across the cracked tile to bump Lauren's feet.

Bending down to pick them up, Lauren tried to reel her temper back in check. But when Markus kicked the bag, the reel snapped. "Well, seeing as you'll spend all the money I make on cheap cigars and poker games within a week, I don't see why I should bother," she muttered.

The kitchen lapsed into the silence dead men were made of.

"… Why you should *bother*?"

Lauren glanced up to meet her brother's burning eyes, and her stomach lurched like ocean waves.

Quickly, she stood and shoved the biscuits onto the table as she stammered a half-baked apology. But the anger in his eyes had him halfway deaf. He picked his way around the kitchen table towards her, his tread slow and dangerous.

"You should *bother*," Markus said, "because without me you wouldn't even be *alive* anymore. *Mom* wouldn't be alive anymore. Skye doesn't accept you, Laur—but Skye loves me. I'm your shield, you see that? If anyone should be working, it should be you, because I can do better things with my time, and you can't." He placed heavy hands on her shoulders and looked her dead in the eyes, like he was paring away her flesh to jab at her soul. "Understand?"

It hurt because he was right.

Lauren couldn't hold his gaze. She chewed on her lip and looked somewhere just beyond his right shoulder—a speckle of sunlight on the kitchen counter. "I understand," she said. The skin of Markus' hands burned through her cardigan. His magic, rejecting her.

Skye magic reminding her that she was not one of Skye's things.

With a con-man's smile, Markus let her go. "Good," he said. "You can try again tomorrow."

Lauren squeezed the edge of her cardigan as he casually picked up and examined the boxed milk.

Then he downed what was left of it in a few quick gulps.

"I'm going to check on Mom," Markus said, putting the box back on the table.

"Okay." Lauren watched a drip of milk slide down the side of the box to wet the table.

His footsteps stomped down the hallway. The bedroom door clicked open, and then clicked shut.

Lauren lurched forward and grabbed the empty milk box, then jammed it into the wastebasket. Her hands shook.

Breathe.

Breathe.

Breathe.

She needed room to breathe.

The Skye air was still cold, and the engine of Lauren's car revved and choked as she tried to start it. And then revved and choked again. Muttering under her breath, Lauren wrapped the trench coat she'd stolen from Markus tighter around her shoulders, and got out to give the hood a strong thump with her fist. She needed to get away before he noticed she was gone.

The engine choked, then gave a temperamental roar and grumbled to life, turning over with a loud creak.

Lauren climbed back into the car and inhaled the smell of dirty leather and coming rain. Soon, she'd be smelling ocean and swan feed. The familiar call of her swans echoed in the back of her head, soothing and calm.

Breathe.

The cobblestones were slick with yesterday's rain under the wheels of her car. When she roared the car off-road, the floor rumbled and jumped beneath her feet as she tore up the near-abandoned dirt road to the crest of the huge, grassy plateau that ended on a cliff which overlooked the ocean and most of Skye.

Lauren pulled the car up next to the pond. It was surrounded by reeds, and the wind brushed them aside like a mother stroking her child's hair. She let the car idle next to the crystal water for a moment before pulling the keys out of the ignition. The engine died dramatically. Lauren slammed the door hard for good measure when she climbed out.

It was good to be alone again.

Shoving her hands into the pockets of Markus' trench coat, Lauren wandered to the other side of the pond, scuffing the thick Skye grass with the soles of her shoes. She might not be one of Skye, but up here she felt like Skye was one of her.

A swan call pierced the sky as Lauren rounded the other side of the lake, and she smiled. She looked up to see the V of her swans flying strong through the air, white feathers ruffling in the breeze as the elegant creatures angled themselves to land in the lake. The sound of their bodies cutting into the water rippled along the pond, and Lauren dug her hand into the inner pocket of the coat she was wearing to pull out the bag of swan feed. It was almost empty. She'd have to get more soon.

If Markus would let her.

Shoving her brother to the back of her mind, Lauren stepped up to the edge of the pond and let the water lap at the toes of her shoes. The grains of feed were familiar against her fingers as she dug her hand inside and tossed it into the water. Ripples purled outward where they landed. Her swans honked loudly, sticking out their necks, strong legs propelling them towards their girl and their food. Good friends they were, Lauren and her swans.

Which was why her brow furrowed when, instead of coming closer to eat out of her hand, the swans stopped three feet away, as if they'd hit a wall, and hissed at her. Water splashed as they beat their large wings. Lauren stumbled backwards, her heart beating faster. Swans were fierce when angered.

"What?" she asked, though they couldn't answer. Their honks grew louder, and she dropped the bag of feed to hold up her hands. "I haven't brought you anything else to eat—that's all there is."

The swans hissed louder, a few of them taking off to dart out of the water. Lauren sucked in a breath and ducked as the largest swan—Timrill—skidded to land behind her, flanked by two others, Velisan and Roeki.

The reeds rustled, murmuring in their whispery voices as Lauren glanced from swan to swan. She knew from one misadventure with the chicks of a swan that their wings were like clubs and their bite left a bruise that lasted a week. Shifting her weight, she eyed her car. Too far away.

Too far to run.

Sighing shakily, she looked at Timrill, who was eyeing her. "I don't have anything else," she said quietly.

A siren's scream echoed through the ocean crashing behind and below them. Timrill's feathers ruffled.

The wind suddenly picked up, smacking Lauren so hard that she yelped and fell to her knees. It was like a hurricane had blown unannounced, tugging her hair and coat and pushing her to the ground. Lauren gasped but couldn't breathe. She ducked her head against the soil and screamed, wondering if she'd be tossed off the plateau and into the rocky sea. If her mother would miss her. If Markus would even notice she was gone.

The wind screamed around her head like a banshee, wailing and crying, a warning to those about to die—

And then it was over.

Lauren breathed hard, the scent of dirt heavy in her nose and her hair a tangled disarray around her head. Shaking, she looked up to see if her swans were gone.

They *were* gone.

In their place stood women.

They were taller than anyone in Skye and their skin was bronzed and clear, black eyes burning in their strong faces. Every woman held a spear and was covered from collarbone to knees in white-feathered garb.

One woman stepped forward, and Lauren recognized her piercing gaze. Timrill.

What had happened to her swans?

"Lauren Dryletski." Timrill spoke in a deep timbre. "We sense foul magic on you. What has happened?"

Lauren opened her mouth to respond, but sudden tears budded in the back of her throat, clogging her voice. Of course, when her swans became something more, they would recognize that she was something less. Of course. "I—I'm sorry," she said, shoving herself into a stand. Beside the goddess-swans, she looked like a tramp. "I'm not—I'm not really one of Skye." A blush rose high in her cheeks. "Who are you?"

Timrill's dark brows dipped low over her sharp eyes, and she stepped forward with a rustle of feathers. It sounded like autumn winds and Skye magic, everything Lauren wanted but could not have. "We are the *selkuno*," she said. "The swan-women who founded Skye, though Skye has forgotten us now. All of Skye but you. We had high hopes for you, Lauren—but now you come to us wearing a pelt so full of foul magic. Why is this?"

Far below, the ocean continued to crash.

High hopes for her? Lauren stammered and tugged at the sleeves of her coat. "It's … not my coat, it's my brother's—" The wind pulled at her flyaway hair, sending a shiver up her spine as she swallowed hard. Her mind couldn't keep up with all their questions. "It's not mine."

Timrill banged the shaft of her spear once against the ground, making Lauren flinch. "Your brother," she barked, an angry hiss underlying her tone as her swan shone through, "carries the magic of a parasite—a foul magic that feeds on others. We can smell it, but we still smell *you*. Why have you not overcome him yet?"

"I don't have magic of my own." Lauren took a step back under the weight of Timrill's gaze, and the pond's reeds brushed the back of her calves. "But he's not a parasite, he's my brother, he's been protecting my Mom and me from getting thrown out of Skye, since we're not really *of* Skye—"

The women behind Timrill hissed when she said it, and Lauren froze in place. Her heartbeat thundered in her chest. Selkies, harpies, banshees she had heard of, but *selkuno*? Were they known to be friendly? Did they feed on human flesh? Would they feed on her?

"This," Timrill said, leveling her spear towards Lauren. Lauren tensed. "This is the work of your brother. This is what a parasite does. He has made you feel worthless and thus sucks your magic away to use it for himself. You *are* one of Skye, Lauren—but more than that, we believe you are meant to be one of the *selkuno*. Your soul is made of Skye. The same as us."

Lauren's heart froze and her blood pumped cold.

Another *selkuno* stepped forward, this one with a few grey feathers in the white of her garb—Roeki. "We invite you to shed your brother's influence and become one of us. Will you accept our invitation, Lauren Dryletski?"

The pond rippled behind her in the wind.

Slowly, almost mechanically, Lauren shook her head. "I don't—I don't think I can."

Though, she wasn't sure exactly what it was she couldn't do. Many things. Many little things that added up to be one large thing—

Lauren Dryletski had no magic.

Lauren Dryletski was not one of Skye.

Rubbing one hand against the chafed wrist of the other, Lauren stared hard at Timrill, and a warm tear dripped down her cheek and turned cold in the wind. "You really think I'm one of Skye?" She asked.

Timrill reached out one dark hand. "Let us show you."

The wind whistled, the only onlooker on the grassy outcropping. It was the only thing watching as Lauren wiped her tears with her knuckles, then reached out with one tear-salted hand to take Timrill's.

Her fingers began to glow.

Encased in Timrill's large palm, Lauren's pale hand gave off a soft white light. It felt how Markus's magic did—warm. But this didn't burn. This wasn't taking.

This was giving.

This was *hers*.

Lauren sucked in a breath and pulled away, looking at her hand. But the glow abruptly stopped when Timrill let go. Flexing her fingers, Lauren tried to bring the feeling back. All she had was the wind and the earth beneath her feet. "What happened?"

Roeki tightened her fist around the shaft of her spear. "Your brother's parasite. You need help to overcome it. You have a magic that gives others strength, Lauren, but your brother has too long stolen it from you. Come with us."

"Come with us," said Timrill.

"Come with us," said the *selkuno*.

I'm one of Skye, Lauren heard.

She flexed her fingers again, then clenched them into fists. She tucked them into the pockets of Markus's coat, and Timrill flinched. Foul magic. A parasite.

Could she escape?

She blew out a thin breath between her lips. "Okay," she said. "On one condition."

The people of Skye saw swans as graceful, delicate, elegant.

The people of Skye who'd ever had the misfortune of being attacked by one of those swans saw them as vicious monsters with wings like small battering rams, and knew their fury was a force to be reckoned with.

And when the *selkuno* puzzled together that Markus the parasite had worked his foul magic on Lauren's mother as well, perfectly trapping both women to the house, their fury was something beyond reckoning.

"Markus?" Lauren stepped into the house but went no further than the front door. The wooden floor creaked—she left the front door open. "Markus—"

"Where were you?" Markus stormed out of the hallway, heading towards her with anger written into the barely-there lines of his smooth Skye face.

Maybe not so Skye anymore.

"You didn't tell me you were leaving," he snapped. "Where did you go?"

"I was—I was visiting some friends." Lauren slowly took off his coat, trying to hide the way her hands were quivering. Maybe this wasn't the right thing to do. Maybe this was another mistake. Maybe she wasn't one of Skye.

She dropped Markus' coat on the threshold.

Markus' gaze flicked down to the coat. His eyes went cold.

But this time, when he strode forward to grab her shoulder and use his parasitical magic, Lauren didn't stand still.

With shaking steps, she backed out of the house onto the front lawn. "Markus, I'm leaving." Her heart stuttered in her chest like a hummingbird dying. She felt like throwing up.

"Lauren—" Markus stepped out after her, his footsteps hard enough to split the earth in two.

But he froze when he found himself surrounded by swans.

Lauren lifted her chin and fought to speak without crying. "Markus, I'm leaving."

Timrill gave her wings an experimental beat and stretched out her long neck, cocking her head at Lauren.

"Yes," Lauren said. "That's him."

Before Markus could speak, the swans launched at him in a tornado of hissing anger and wings like clubs. Ducking around the mob, Lauren dashed into the house and ran to her mother's bedroom.

"Mom—" Lauren skidded to the bedside and almost collapsed. Everything was trembling. Eyes wide with worry, her mother struggled to sit up, and Lauren took her hand. "I found a way for us to get out. Both of us."

Her mother shook her head, tears forming in her eyes. "Not strong enough," she mouthed.

Lauren's breath came fast and short. Her voice was a whisper stolen by the stale air of the room. "Mom, I think I have magic. Magic that gives people strength. I think ... I might be able to help you."

A single tear trickled down her mother's cheek.

It was that tear that fueled Lauren.

Taking a deep breath, she dug in her soul for the warmth that Timrill had awakened on the windy cliff. For the magic that Markus had taken away for so long.

And slowly, shakily, brokenly, she poured strength into the person she loved most in all the world.

Timrill, a woman once more, helped walk Lauren's mother out of the house and guided her into Lauren's car for the drive back to the cliff. Lauren packed a small bag for both of them—they wouldn't need much to start their lives over. The *selkuno* would take care of them.

Stepping outside in her kitten-heeled shoes, Lauren saw that they had very aptly taken care of Markus.

He sat leaning against the front of the house, nursing bruised ribs and glaring at the *selkuno* standing guard around the car. Lauren paused on the crooked front porch, looking at him. His sullen gaze darted to her face.

"Well?" He spat blood on the ground. One of his teeth was missing.

Lauren shook her head. Then she dropped her packed bag down next to him. He would need it more than she or her mother would. "Bye, Markus."

She could feel his eyes on her all the way to the car. She could feel his eyes on her as she smiled at their mother and planted a kiss on her thin cheek before turning the key in the ignition. She could feel his eyes on her as the car drove towards the ocean and a sky full of swans soared after them in a strong V.

And then the house was far behind them.

And she couldn't feel his eyes anymore.

"Watch your step, Mom."

Lauren walked beside her mother towards the pond above the ocean, one arm wrapped around her shoulders. Her mother's pace was unsteady, but a wondering smile spread as wide as the ocean across her face.

Lauren, though her own smile was rusted with disuse, smiled back.

The *selkuno* stood at the edge of the grassy cliff, looking out at the sea, the rustling white feathers of their garb the only part of them in motion. Lauren and her mother paused behind them, arms around each other—mother and daughter, one creature.

One creature of Skye.

They took a deep breath.

"We're ready," said Lauren.

The *selkuno* turned around, and Timrill stepped forward. A smile graced her bronze face as she tapped the shaft of her spear against the ground. In response to her prompting, every other *selkuno* slowly spread around Lauren and her mother, tapping their spears against the ground as they encircled them. A wind picked up, fierce and all-encompassing.

Lauren looked at her mother—her eyes were happy and full of tears.

The *selkuno* began a chant as the wind grew stronger. It tugged at their feathers and flapped Lauren's clothes against her body. The chanting grew into a storm. Lauren closed her eyes against the strength of it all and squeezed her mother's shoulders—

The *selkuno* gave a shout and banged their spears against the ground.

Everything fell dead silent.

And then Lauren felt the change.

It started in her bones, a warm hum and then a tingle in the pit of her stomach. It felt like remembering something she'd lost. Her legs longed to propel her into the air and never land again. There was a fast, sweeping sensation over her skin, like being submerged underwater all at once. Lauren gasped.

When she opened her eyes, she was dressed in white.

The *selkuno's* feathered garb cloaked her body, white feathers ruffling in the breeze. A spear was gripped tight in her hand. The urge to run and throw herself off the cliff and into the lifting wind nearly overtook her, the call of the swans bubbling in her chest. But Lauren tucked it back and turned to look at—

Her mother.

Her mother looked so *strong*.

Her lined face was smoother, and her hands didn't shake as she studied the gleaming spear that now belonged to her. Her glowing eyes met Lauren's.

"Baby girl," she whispered.

Lauren let out a gasp like a cry and threw her arms around her mother's neck. Her fingers flickered with magic—*her* magic made for giving strength—and her mother took a deep breath. Lauren smiled so hard it hurt.

She was one of Skye.

"Are you ready to fly?" Timrill's mellow voice rang clear across the pond.

Lauren pulled away from her mother and looked at Timrill. The cloudy sky spread clear and open and free, wider than any dream she'd ever had. "We're ready," she said.

Timrill lifted her spear, and as one creature the *selkuno* began to run.

Across the grass, impossibly fast, the beat of their feet a tribal call, they ran to the edge of the cliff and threw themselves off toward the sea. But instead of crashing, they were caught in the wind. Their arms became wings, and their bodies became birds, and they shot into the sky.

Lauren's heart soared in her chest.

Without pausing to consider, she tore off, feet pounding the ground and blood rush-rush-rushing through her veins. The wind was a siren, and she responded to its song.

She leapt from the cliff into the air.

A jubilant cry tore from her lips as her skin became feathers and the air became her home, but then it wasn't a cry at all—it was a swan-call, and the *selkuno* responded in kind. And above them all trumpeted the call of her mother. A glow of happiness exploded in Lauren's chest.

She'd never heard her sound so alive.

Flapping her newfound wings, Lauren glided into the strong V of the *selkuno*, right beside her mother. The wind lifted them higher, higher, higher, and her magic pulsed to the reckless beat of her heart.

She was one of them.

One of Skye.

Lauren cried the *selkuno's* call, and it rang through the wind and wheeled in her soul.

She was free.

Nothing More Than Death

Beka Gremikova

The sickroom is in a state of disarray. Chamber pots line the side of Prince Seth-Jairin's bed for the moments his bowels lose control. Master Oro-kor, the lead physician of the royal family, directs the servants to remove the full chamber pots and bring fresh ones in. Prince Seth-Jairin lies still on the bed, choking on each breath, wheezing like a cat with its ribs kicked in.

One maid stands to the side, her only duty to clutch the traditional death shroud of Bevrin in her arms as they all await the final moments. The soft blue silk is meant to reflect the colorful serenity of the Second World. As soon as the prince breathes his last, she will lay the shroud over his chest, leaving his face bare to respect his rank. It is meant to be an honor, but the maid looks ill.

At the head of the bed, Queen Deme-tra and her husband lean over their son. The queen strokes his forehead while King Thral-kor smooths out the wrinkles in his son's blanket and tucks it around his legs. Opposite the royals, Life herself holds the prince's hand, unseen by the humans but for Prince Seth-Jairin and the physician.

"My sister, Fate, has given you to me," she says, clasping his fingers. The vibrancy of her golden glow reflects in his skin as his body fights against the illness. She wishes the king and queen could see her, could know that their son will make it through. Life settles on the bedsheet, reaching out to caress the Seth-Jairin's cheek.

He does not stir at her touch, does not even blink. Life puffs out her lips, nerves gnawing at her stomach. This cannot mean—

She hears distant, echoing screams and stiffens as a familiar presence approaches behind her. With a half-turn, she faces Death. Death, the youngest of the many Universal Sisters, wears the same soft sky blue as the Bevrin shroud, but there is no peace to be seen in the fabric. Each fold holds a dream broken by her presence, and every decorative silver deckle reflects a life cut short by her hand. The awful voices of lost souls scream out from the cloth.

Life presses her hands to her ears, casting her sister a narrowed look. From where he stands, Master Oro-kor gives a short gasp.

Death gives a slight cough, and the wails, though not cut off, lower to a less noticeable pitch. "I do not have the power to cut them off," she says. "That is beyond my grasp. I can only remind them that they cannot be found, so why scream so loudly?"

At the sound of Death's voice, Seth-Jairin stirs, his eyes creaking open. A sticky-looking glaze crusts the corners of his sockets, while the same substance coats his lips. As he locks eyes with Death, Life feels her sway over him trickle away.

Death feels the moment Seth-Jairin's gaze falls on her. His breath hitches and his dark brown skin breaks out in bumps. As he sinks back into his pillows, his breathing labored, his mother snatches his hand. Frantic murmurs course through the servants.

"What happens if His Highness dies?" Death looks to the maid holding the shroud as she inches closer to Master Oro-Kor, as though his authority can relieve her trepidation. "Will there be civil war if the king and queen can't have another child? It was bad enough when poor Al-yen died—"

"Hush," Master Oro-Kor snaps. "There are steps to take in finding another to inherit the crown," he adds in a more reassuring tone when the maid's eyes fill with tears. But his eyes dart to the king and queen. The queen is looking at him.

"What has happened?" Usually it would come out as a sharp

demand, but grief has pummeled the hardness from her voice. When Queen Deme-tra was but twenty-five, her mother followed Death into the Second World. The queen had lost much of her sharpness then, too, and the only thing that brought any of it back was her marriage and queenship. Death wonders if this loss will break Prince Seth-Jairin's mother entirely.

"Do you need me to tell you?" Master Oro-kor asks. His rigid shoulders tell all—he does not want to have to say it.

"Death is here," the queen murmurs. She has lain herself out beside her son, and her breaths come in deep, choking gulps as she struggles not to sob.

"Seth-Jairin," she whispers.

"*Malyin*," he croaks. It is a pet name, the name a child calls his mother. Queen Deme-tra presses her cheek against his skin.

"Oh, my *yin-mal*." She uses the Bevrin term for an unborn child, one still protected by his mother's womb.

"There is nothing more we can do," Master Oro-kor says. He glances at the king, who nods.

"You cannot protect him anymore, Deme-tra," King Thral-kor says, gripping his wife's shoulder. "And you cannot wait any longer. I don't wish you to see—" He breaks off, his voice hitching.

The last breath.

Death averts her gaze, meeting the eyes of her sister across the bed.

Life's golden glow flares in rage. "Why are you here?"

Death inclines her head toward the prince. "Fate has given me Seth-Jairin," she murmurs. She wishes she could speak mind to mind with her Sister, but neither Death nor Life are allowed to hide or embellish the truth from those they serve. Fate, as the eldest, rarely speaks to mortals at all.

Despite her attempt to lower her voice, Seth-Jairin hears her words.

A shudder courses through him, and an agonized cry escapes his lips. His mother throws her arms around him, drawing him close, sobbing into his neck. His father sways on his feet.

"Out," Master Oro-kor snaps. "All of us. Say your goodbyes. Now." The servants all but dash out the door.

The queen collects herself enough to press a kiss to Seth-Jairin's forehead.

"Though Death approaches, may Life yet prevail," King Thralkor murmurs to his son, a final blessing and a desperate wish.

Both king and queen drag their steps as Master Oro-Kor ushers them away. Even they cannot disobey an order from the physician, who, in cases of illness and death, has been given ultimate authority in Bevrin.

"How can Fate be so fickle?" Life explodes.

Death shrugs. "I do not know her mind. Did you have such brilliant plans for his future?" As soon as Death utters the words, she wishes she could bite her tongue. Life does not appreciate sarcasm, and the last thing Death wants is to have Life as an enemy. Though they are natural rivals, they often must work alongside each other in the same space, Life reviving, Death revolving lives into the Second World. A battlefield is often their mutual ground.

"I apologize," she says as Life's chin quivers.

Life bends over the prince. "Remember your parents. Remember how your aunt and uncle mourned the loss of Al-yen. Remember your kingdom, the wars you must win for them." At that, Seth-Jairin flinches. Life lifts his chin and presses her lips to one of his cheeks, then his forehead, and then his other cheek, completing the circle of blessing of Unersa, the far eastern empire she has been trying to reclaim from its death and disease for centuries. "Fate is indeed fickle, oh prince. She may yet change her mind—and when she does, I'll be waiting to rescue you." She straightens, flickering a withering glance at Death as she passes by.

Death takes Life's place beside the prince, standing by the bed. She realizes with a bit of a start that time has flickered past with its usual speed, leaving her impressions twisted. She remembers Seth-Jairin last as a laughing boy of thirteen who fell off his horse and nearly died from his injuries.

Now his skin is hardened with fine lines of both laughter and sorrow. The plump cheeks of the boy are replaced by the sharp contours of the man. The man who should have become a king.

"Hello," she says softly. She brushes her fingers against his cheek.

He leans into her touch, his eyelashes fluttering.

"This should be a warrior's death," he croaks out. He struggles to sit up. "I don't want you to see me wasting away." He leans closer, his lips thinning and drying out as the inches decrease between them. His breath stirs against her thick, dark eyelashes as he lifts a hand to stroke her face. She flinches at his touch, which, despite his illness, is still so warm, so full of life and vigor.

"This is a warrior's death," she says. "To live day after day, suffering ... it is not 'the easy way.' And to watch it unfold takes a warrior's heart." She nods to his mother, who lingers in the doorway, her fingers gripping the frame. Queen Deme-tra's eyes blaze with grief and a fierce love that defies that grief. A fierce love that keeps watching for any signs of life and a fierce hope even when her heart cannot bear to witness that last breath.

The queen's shoulders quiver. Death knows she's thinking of watching her own mother die, wasting away with a quickness that took their family by surprise. Queen Deme-tra had been old enough that people assumed she no longer needed a mother—but Death knew it was just when she'd lost her that the queen needed her mother more than ever.

"Not you too," the queen whispers. "I'm not ready—I need you. My baby." She sobs. "*Malyin!*" She cries out for her own mother, sinking to her knees. "Why did I have to lose you, and now I must lose my son?" She wraps her arms around herself, weeping, just as she did that day twenty-five years ago. Then, she'd been alone in her chambers sobbing into her pillows. Now she weeps and speaks openly, unashamed of her grief, challenging her husband and physician trying to coax her out of the room to try to tell her it isn't as bad as it looks.

As her mourning sinks into the souls of those around her, nobody can say a word. Her husband kneels beside her, wrapping his arms around her shoulders. He presses his face into her neck. Tears stream down her cheeks. Even as she leans into him, her eyes seem to stare right at Death, glazed and vulnerable.

"Would you have him die a warrior's death?" Death murmurs to Queen Deme-tra even though the prince's mother cannot hear her. She glances down at Seth-Jairin. He meets her gaze, his own frightened yet assured. "Do you want to be torn to pieces on a battlefield?"

He flinches. "I ... never wanted that," he says, the truth slipping out of him.

"Of course not," Death says. "A man's best shield is his bravado." She perches on the edge of the bed, peering over her shoulder. To her relief, Life stands between the king and queen, exuding comfort. From where she stands, Death can feel it—a sensation like an invisible embrace and soft, murmured words weaving through her hair. She watches as the king and queen waver in Life's presence and allow Master Oro-kor to finally lead them away from the sickroom. *Even when your heart is dying,* Death thinks, *life drags you on whether you want it to or not.*

She is grateful to her sister. Death hates having an audience for her work. The stress and sorrow of the atmosphere is straining and distracting. It is difficult to woo with so many people watching.

Silence falls but for Seth-Jairin's gasping and the drip of rain through the cracks in the ceiling.

She realizes Seth-Jairin's hand is still on her face, and his eyes, though glazed, are steady on hers. "I was dying," he says. "And you came. You let me go. Twice, when I was younger."

"I cannot take credit for that. My Sister Fate decreed it. I would not have let you go if I could help it."

"And now she says I must go with you?" He asks.

She nods. "Are you ready?"

He bites out a laugh. "Is anyone ever ready?"

"Some are," she says.

"Like Al-yen," he murmurs. His fingers flicker from her face to her hair, burying themselves amongst the strands. "I found her smiling. You were kind to her."

"Kindness is not a word that applies to death," she says. "It is a mortal construct."

"Dung," he retorts. "Most of us wouldn't know kindness if it hit us in the face."

"Fine. Kindness is a requirement for me."

"Dung again." He juts out his chin. "I've seen criminals suffer horrid deaths. You don't soothe them. But you care for children, for those like Al-yen."

Al-yen. Death tilts her head back, remembering. A child with the brown curls and wide smile of the prince. She had wondered about their relation. Al-yen had been an easy steal; she'd followed Death's whispers with a satisfied sigh. She had not feared the Second World. "You are very much like her."

"Thank you," he wheezes. "It helps." He pauses. "If I must die, may I ask one request?"

"Of course," Death says. Final requests have become quite popular amongst Bevrin nobility in recent years, as though they might prolong the inevitable until Death gives up on them and releases them from her clutches. "A final request is usually given, if I'm able to fulfill it."

"This is mine," he says, and takes her hand to pull her towards him until she rests against his chest. He snakes one arm around her waist while his other hand cups her neck, forcing her head to angle. She realizes what he's about to do and sighs inwardly. He is hardly the first, and he certainly won't be the last man who falls for his own demise. How many young men, though full of life, have still written about the arms of Death encircling them in the poetic romance of demise? How many of them have dreamed darkly of her, using her as an escape from life?

His nose brushes against her cheek, and his eyelashes flutter as he sighs. His lips are but a breath from hers when his gaze shifts to the door. His eyes glaze and his lips twist. The prince sits back with a huff, a deep frown digging into his brow.

Released, Death steps away as quickly and subtly as she can. "You're confused," she says.

"My parents." His voice falters. "I can't just leave my mother."

Death shakes her head. "You have no choice," she says softly. "Fate has decreed it."

"Do *you* ever get a choice?"

She smiles. "I don't know if you will understand," she says, "but my will is different from that of humans. You think of it as something you alone can own. My will is communal—it must be in harmony with both Life and Fate in order to keep History going and appeased. We do not always agree with or like our decisions, but we all know these decisions must be seen through."

"You aren't human?" He straightens, piercing her with his glance. "Are you upset?"

He twists his bedsheets in his hands. Then, catching notice of the shroud, he kicks it off the bed. "I suppose you've had your share of princes falling for you," he says.

"Not as many as you might think," Death says. "Most princes try to run the other way." She chuckles before she adds, "You must not love me before the proper time and out of the proper manner. There is a saying like that in the Holy Bevrin Annunciations, is there not?"

He bows his head, abashed. "Indeed," he murmurs.

"I do not say this out of spite," she says. "But to love Death more than one ought … it does not bode well for one's mind. Healthy respect is necessary, but do not feed your yearnings."

He tilts his head. "But what if I love you not because you're Death, but because I want you to stay. To be more. To be—" He breaks off.

"Human?" she asks.

"Why can't you? Can't you love?"

About to settle back on the edge of the bed, she thinks better of it and remains standing. She grips the clasps of her cloak in her fingers, the cool metal giving her purpose to fight his wheedling. She has found humans attractive before, and this will not be the last time. "I am part of a created order," she says, "just as you are. It's not so much that I do not have desires to leave my lot—but that I physically cannot. I am *nothing more* than death." She points to her eyes, the bright, marbled yellow-green of the precious gems mined in the Bevrin deserts. "Every part of me that appears human is merely that—*appearance*. I appear human because I am a *reflection* of humanity, which is the pinnacle of the Creator's order. I am kind to children and full of judgement for criminals because those are *reflections*, however imperfect, of the One who made me. My love is that of the sun withering the grass so new growth can replace it. For me, romantic love can exist only in this realm, for it does not belong in the Second

World." She grasps his reaching hand tightly, not sure if she should crush his fingers like a soldier or enfold them like a beloved. She settles for the firmness of a friend. "Now, as Fate has decreed, Seth-Jairin of Bevrin, follow me into—"

With a sudden tenseness, she realizes the rain has stopped dripping from the ceiling. Sunshine filters through the gauzy curtains of the prince's sick room, even though it is the middle of the night. A glowing presence approaches, vibrant and humming a victory tune. The scuff of skipping steps echoes in the far hallway of the palace. Death's knees buckle, and she swallows the urge to gag.

"It—it appears Fate has changed her mind once more," she says. "And, from my sister's dancing walk, she has changed it for the last time."

"You're leaving?" Seth-Jairin's eyes widen in alarm. He tries to tug her to him, but she resists.

"You should be relieved," she says sharply and leans over to slap his cheek.

His hand rises to his face as he snaps back, "Relieved that I can die a horrid death on a battlefield?"

"You have been very blessed by the Creator thus far. Have I not brought down many of your enemies in the battlefield?" She says this to assure herself as much as him. For all the man's silly notions, he has valor and a deep love for his parents that she cannot help but admire. She does not wish to see him butchered like a pig, surrounded by mud and blood—

Enough. Fate's voice, ringing with the authority given to her by their Creator, pushes the images from Death's mind. *Sister, I have called you back. You cannot save him from a gruesome death on the battlefield if it is Decreed.*

I will come, Death says. *Why is it so unfair?*

This entire world is unfair, dear sister. It is not what it once was—but take comfort that we know our purpose and our plan. Not all humans can say so. You are Death, I am Fate, and neither of us can change that. You were created for a purpose just as the prince was. Now, tell him to be ready for Life. Fate's voice fades from Death's mind.

"Why can't you live, stay—" Seth-Jairin is saying.

"Good-bye, my prince," she says. She feels heavy. She bends over to brush her lips against his forehead. His hand splays across her neck, his palm rough with callouses. He gently angles her head. He murmurs, "I didn't get my final request."

"You're going to live. Men who live don't get final requests. But this isn't good-bye, Seth-Jairin," she says. "This is 'until we meet again.'"

"Then I'd like to say that for myself." His grip is firm, his tone pleading.

She relents and her fingers curl into his tunic as his mouth finds hers. The life throbbing in his veins consumes her with sensations of salt and light, the warmth in his skin battling the coldness of death in her fingers until her limbs begin to go weak.

His hands drop to her wrists, his thumbs pressing into her skin to feel for a pulse. Laughter tickles her stomach at his desperation to make her seem human, but her body plays along, her arms wrapping around his neck. He kisses her again, a needy kiss that begs her to stay with him forever.

Her yearning to stay has been steadily increasing, and with it her annoyance. "I am Death. Death cannot Live, even if a prince orders her to," she reminds him.

Seth-Jairin merely smiles and kisses her again. Her eyes flutter closed, but then a tugging sensation snags her attention. His hands are on the clasps of her cloak, as though by casting the cloak from her shoulders he will free her from her own existence. For a moment, she contemplates letting him do so, letting him guide her footsteps and her whims.

His knuckles brush against her collarbone, and the warmth that flares out is too much for her. *You are part of a created order*, she tells herself. *Your place, your existence, is far greater than one man's desire and your own temptation. Temptation has nothing to give you but a brief escape from truth.*

She slaps his hands away and sits back sharply. "Even if a king declares it," she says, "Death cannot Live. And you will make a wonderful king."

She rubs a hand along her tingling collarbone as the sensation slowly dies away. "You have much living left to do. There are others who need someone familiar with grief and death. Do you understand?"

After a moment of wide-eyed shock, consideration returns to the prince's gaze and he nods.

"There is more to life than death, Seth-Jairin," she says. "And there is more to death than trying to reassure yourself it won't hurt too much by thinking you're in love with me. You and I shall meet again soon enough, but once Life is gone, you will not meet her again in the same fashion. I will have you until the coming of the Third World, she but for a mere seventy years." She licks her lips. "Be kind to her. Though it doesn't always seem like it, she is your ally as much as I."

"Then why is she so difficult?" His eyes glint.

"You're asking why Life is difficult?" Death asks. She grins despite herself. "I shall have to remember to ask Fate to give you your lot on a silver platter."

He glares at her, but it's lost as the door opens and Master Oro-Kor pokes his head in. His lips are thinned, his eyes glistening. When he sees Seth-Jairin, propped up in bed, still breathing, he steps full into the room. Life sweeps past him, her face radiant. She wraps her arms around Seth-Jairin's neck. Health glows in the prince's cheeks. The physician approaches, his gaze darting between Life and Death, as though uncertain which one to believe. He grasps the prince's arm to check his pulse.

Death stands and inclines her head toward the door, indicating that she is about to leave. She crosses her arms in front of her chest, the silent sign that she will not be returning in this battle.

The physician's lips part, and a croak of joy escapes. The pain and weariness of his job falls from him. He turns and almost bursts out of the room.

"As difficult as Life can be," Death says, with a teasing glance at her sister before becoming somber again, "it has its moments of grace to ease the grief. Look, Seth-Jairin, your mother is coming."

Once more the door opens and the queen flies in, her skirts tangling around her legs as she collapses beside Seth-Jairin. The prince's breath catches, and Death knows he's forgotten all about Life and Death and Fate as he wraps his mother in his arms. She cries into his neck.

"I'll survive," he says to her, rubbing soothing patterns against her back. "I'll survive, *Malyin*." As he says it, determination settles in his eyes, and they almost seem to sparkle in the light of the candles. He glances at Death. "I may have fallen for Death," he says, his voice tight. His gaze slides to Life on the other side. "But that doesn't mean I cannot appreciate Life for her friendship and all the chances found therein." Relief flits across his features. Death can see that whatever feelings he may have for her, and whatever her love for him might look like, he is glad he doesn't have to die.

Queen Deme-tra pulls back from him, cupping his face in her hands. She cannot speak, so she simply stares at her son as she weeps.

Death smiles as Life stretches between the queen and her son. Her sister's eyes shine. Instead of defeat, Death merely feels anticipation—she is the most patient amongst her sisters.

"I leave him to you," she says to Life. "Treat him well, sister."

"I will treat him as well I can," Life says. "As long as Fate decrees."

Death nods.

Life picks up the shroud from the floor and gives it to Death. "Take this with you. Burn it for me."

"No," Death says, her voice thoughtful. "I think I shall keep it awhile. It would make a lovely cloak." She catches Master Oro-Kor's eye as he returns with the king. She lifts the shroud with a questioning raise of her eyebrow. The physician confers with the king, and then he nods at her.

"It is a gift of thanks," Life says. "They think you had some sort of choice in the matter."

Death sighs. "Sometimes, I wish I did." But at other times, she admits, she feels oddly glad she is merely following orders. She glances down once more at Seth-Jairin, and then she is gone, the silk shroud wrapped around her shoulders.

Life shrugs out of her golden cloak and drapes it across Seth-Jairin's chest as his mother bids him to sleep. He passes out quickly, his brow clear of the furrows of illness. His mother joins his father and together they leave, their whispers low and full, not the broken, uncertain mutters of grief.

This victory belongs to Life, if only for a time. Then, it will be Death's turn, until the Third World comes, all begins anew, and Death is longer needed.

I will take care of him, Sister, Life says softly. Although physically her sister is gone, she can feel her lingering. *And one day, he'll be all yours.*

Seth-Jairin sighs in his sleep.

I will be waiting, Death answers.

Isn't It Cruel?

Kristina Mahr

Death could not be certain, but he thought he had a thing for blondes.

He mulled this over at length as he was called to his next assignment. He wondered at things like height and eye color and age, things he had never cared enough to parse out before. All he had ever really cared about where humans were concerned was how many grains of sand were left in their hourglass, and, specifically, whether they were down to their last one. Now that he was considering it, though, he could not believe there was such variety. Why, there were short women with long hair, tall women with short hair, brown-eyed girls with red hair, and blue-eyed girls with black hair. A truly endless, bottomless array, and who was to say that any one was better than any other? How on Earth did any human choose one over another?

It was a daunting task, this, and he thought how lucky Hades had been to simply have been handed Persephone for his wife. Death had nobody to gift him much of anything, let alone a bride, so when he had set his mind to this chore, he had known he would bear its full weight.

As he bore everything.

As he never could share even an ounce of his burdens, and as burdens go, Death carried a considerable one.

Though it wasn't until lately that he thought he might like to share it.

It had struck him out of the blue one night — a full moon of a night, perhaps that was to blame—as he had escorted one soul younger than most to its next destination, and it had lodged itself rather annoyingly into his mind. He could not unthink it once he thought it, a quicksand of a thought, and so, at last, he had resolved to stop fighting against its pull.

Death would find himself a Persephone.

He had thought that this decision would be the most difficult part, after an eternity of living, no, *existing*, on his own, but here he was, studying elderly women and young coeds, married women and spinsters, and no, that had been the easy part. *This* was the impossible part. None seemed right, or they all seemed right. He wasn't quite sure which.

Was there some sort of sign humans looked for in a mate? He had been present at enough deathbeds to know of the existence of love, though he was not sure how one recognized it. Was it simply a decision? If one had a thing for blondes, did they pick one and declare their love? He was uncertain, and growing increasingly testy in his uncertainty, for he had never had cause to be uncertain before.

He dealt in certainties. There was nothing more certain than death, and so, there was no one more certain than Death.

It was under the weight of this testiness that he prowled into the hospital room to fetch his latest charge and caught a glimpse of the back of Mae Lawrence's neck. He was struck at once by the curve of it, by the wisping strands of night-black hair curling against it from where they had escaped her bun, by the slender fragility of it. It made him vaguely nauseous, to think how easily it could be broken. Ah, humans. So small and weak and mortal.

But, he had to acknowledge, as he came around the side of her, capable of such beauty.

It was something he had surprisingly never been forced to acknowledge before.

But it was there before him, in Mae Lawrence's bowed neck and in her small nose and in her blue-green eyes that shimmered and swam and overflowed with tears, and, yes, Death who dealt in certainties was quite certain this was beauty.

Well, then, he thought.
Well, then.
Perhaps this was how one chose.

He had a hundred other places to be, at this precise second, and the last grain of sand was shaking itself free from the hourglass of the old man over whom Mae Lawrence cried, but she was saying something, reciting something from a piece of crinkled paper clutched in her shaking hands. Death decided he could spare a moment or two or three.

He could not, but he decided that he could.

He stood in the doorway, seemingly frozen in time, as he listened to her read:

Every time I count my loves,
my losses are just as high,
for every hello has to it chained
an inevitable goodbye.

I flinch at every sunrise,
knowing how soon it will once more set,
and I could not float from the ground for hope,
for fear is as weighted as anchors can get.

It is hard to sift through ashes
when you remember them as flames,
and it is impossible to sleep at night
when all that's left is an echo of their names.

There are bruises on my knees from where
I've dropped to them and begged,
from where I've grasped at the paper edges of time
and attempted to wrest promises upon which it has inevitably reneged.

I am missing, and I have missed,
and in between, I simply miss.

*Life surrounds me here in wreckage where
I once stood wrapped in bliss.*

And isn't it cruel —

Yes, Death thought to himself. *Yes*.
He found he could not bear to hear the rest, in her low and shaky tone, the ink blotting and blurring beneath her tears, and so with a delicate tug, he pulled the old man free of his crippled body. The machines in the room instantly protested, and nurses rushed in. Mae Lawrence let out the smallest of sounds, half keen, half sigh, wholly heartbreak, as Death wished he could tell her he was sorry.

He, who was never sorry.

He, who had not known that seeing someone else's heart break could inspire one's own to shift and shatter.

He, who had not been sure he even had a heart, no, who was quite sure he did not, except he could have sworn he felt something happen in the region of his chest.

It took him no time at all to escort the old man to his next destination, half the time it usually did, for he hurried.

He never hurried, but he hurried.

He returned to the hospital to find the room emptied of people, emptied of Mae Lawrence in particular, though he had enough otherworldliness within him to enable him to find her in the hospital gardens. To enable him to find her there, alone, sitting on a bench as the sun fell toward the horizon, the wind freeing more and more strands of her hair until, with Death watching, it tumbled free.

And now Death was even more sure that there was something in his chest, for now it pulled him forward.

For now, he had no desire to stop it.

Perhaps this, after all, was how humans chose their mates.

By a pull in their chest, and no desire to stop it.

Death thought this might be called wanting.

He *wanted*.

He had never wanted before.

He quickly assembled himself into something he thought might please her. Fair hair to contrast her dark strands, warm brown eyes, some degree of height, a lean figure, a tilt of a smile. He shoved the sleeves of a black sweater up to his elbows and wondered if perhaps he should have chosen a suit. But he was in the act of being pulled, and so, it was too late to change his mind. Black sweater, dark jeans, a tilt of a smile.

He hoped it would be enough.

"Is anyone sitting here?" He kept his voice low and gentle, careful not to startle her, though she looked startled all the same to look up and find him there.

She shook her head wordlessly and gestured at the empty seat beside her, tucking her newly freed hair behind her ears.

Death sat and followed her gaze out to the setting sun. He thought of her poem, about the inevitability of it, about how everything ends, everything goes.

He thought, *how grateful she will be to be freed of it all.*

But of course, he could not lead with that.

"Are you okay?" He asked in that same careful tone, the kind intended to dent silence rather than shatter it. The kind silence could open and close around, the smallest of interruptions, not enough to scare it fully away.

Not enough to scare *her* fully away.

He knew enough about humans to know that they feared him.

She cleared her throat and shook her head. "My grandfather just died."

Grandfather. Yes, that explained the way the old man's eyes had been just as blue and just as green in his youth as Mae Lawrence's were right now. It explained the way, once upon a time, his hair had been black like hers instead of white. Death could see the familial resemblance.

"I am terribly sorry," he said, because he knew that's what was expected of him, because that's what humans said, but also because, in this case, he had been the one to bring it about. Though the order came from a place far beyond him, a place where hourglasses were granted only a set number of grains of sand. He really had no say in it, no, he had no control over it, no, he was just the executor — nonetheless, he had been the one to cut the old man's tether to the earth.

And so, he meant it when he said that he was sorry.

He did not like to have contributed to the tears still gathering in her eyes.

"He was old," Mae said in a stilted tone, continuing to give the horizon the whole of her attention. "But at least he's at peace now."

Death nodded slowly. "Yes. Yes, he is that."

He was that. Death had escorted him to it himself. Had placed his hand into the light, had delivered him unto peace.

Something in his tone drew Mae's full attention at last, and when she turned to face him, Death was hardly prepared for it. Something inside of him opened, a door he had not known he possessed. He wondered if it might lead somewhere. He wondered if it might lead everywhere.

"Life is so fleeting," he said to the ocean of her eyes. "So cruel."

She reared back, away, and Death cursed himself a fool for whatever he had said to cause it. Still, it was only what she'd said earlier, in her poem. She believed it, even if she shook her head at him right now.

"Oh, it's not," she said, more strength in her voice than he had yet heard. "It's not cruel."

"Isn't it?" He lifted an eyebrow, a trick he was grateful this body allowed him. "You ... I mean, *we* live and then we die. Don't you sometimes wonder at how meaningless it all is? Don't you wonder what the point is?"

No meaning, no point. He was sure she'd see it, that she'd cave beneath the weight of it, that she'd welcome his proposition when it came. Instead, she shook her head.

"Oh, no, I don't wonder at all. I know what the point of it is."

She smiled, and he thought, *well, hell.*

He didn't think the thought often, but he thought the thought now, in the face of her smile. If ever there was a time to draw a smile to the devil's face at the mention of his home, it was now, in the face of her smile.

Though he supposed it would have been more apt to think, *well, heaven*.

Well, heaven, with its blinding light and pearly gates, with its peace and its ease and its warm welcome.

"Enlighten me, then," he said, when he remembered how to speak.

She tilted her head at him, her tears receding so that all her eyes held were questions. "Do you really not know?"

He shook his head silently, for he really did not know.

"Just … just look out there." She gestured toward the sun, toward what was left of it, as pinks and purples and oranges came out to pay final respects. "Have you ever seen anything more beautiful?"

He looked from the sky to her and back again and thought it might be a trick question.

"And oh, look at the lilies," she said, thankfully not waiting for an answer, pointing at the flowers that surrounded them. "And the roses. How can you be mad at a world that makes roses that shade of red?"

He looked at the roses in question and shrugged.

"They don't serve much of a purpose. They don't stop anyone from getting sick, or getting hurt, or dying."

"Oh," Mae said, shaking her head. "Not everything needs to have a big, grand purpose. Sometimes their purpose can just be to be beautiful. To move you."

"To move you where?"

She threw back her head and laughed at that, and Death would have been utterly enraptured by the sound had he not also been confused as to what had sparked it.

"Just … to *move* you. You know, to make you feel."

Death was second-guessing this entire enterprise. Sure, she was beautiful and forced him to consider, for the first time, that he might be in possession of a heart, but he could not for the life of himself understand her.

"What good is feeling something when it's inevitably going to end?"

"Haven't you ever been in love?" She turned more fully on the bench to face him. "I'm sorry, I don't even know you. I know that's a crazy question to ask a total stranger, but … haven't you? Haven't you ever felt something that you look back upon and are glad you felt, even if you no longer feel it?"

Death shook his head silently. No, he was not sure he had even *felt*, let alone looked back upon a feeling. Until today, he supposed, when a door had opened and he thought that door might be a feeling.

"You've never felt happiness, even if its fleeting? Something that picked you up and moved you, and made you feel like you were lighter than air, like you could float clear up into the clouds?"

Death shook his head again. "I've never felt happiness."

"Oh," she said, sounding sorry. *Her*, sounding sorry for *him*. Death could not fathom it. "That's dreadful. I'm sorry that you've never felt it."

"But because I've never felt it, I've never had to feel the end of it," he countered. "I've never had to deal with loss, with heartbreak, with wretched, bone-deep sadness."

She sighed long and low, eyes dropping to her tangled hands for a moment before lifting back up to meet his. He was struck anew by the depth of them. By how she could not be more than twenty, and yet, for all of his eons of existence, he was not sure he had depth in him to match hers. "You know, I'm sad right now. Terribly, terribly sad. My grandfather was such a large part of my life, and I'm going to miss him an unfathomable amount. But it doesn't mean I would trade the years I had with him. It doesn't mean I'd ever wish away all of the good memories, just to rid myself of the bad ones. It is worth the pain to have loved him."

Death felt frustration billowing within himself.

"But I *heard* you recite your poem," he told her, bracing one arm along the back of the bench as he faced her in earnest. "I was nearby, and I heard you read it to your grandfather, and I *know* how painful life is. I know that you feel that pain, that it weighs you. I know that you agree that life is cruel."

Mae's brow furrowed for a moment like a quickly passing rainstorm before clearing abruptly into sunshine skies. "Oh … *oh*. You didn't hear the end of it, then. I didn't get to the end of it."

Death's own brow collapsed as he shook his head. "I'm sure it was only more along the same vein."

"It wasn't." Mae reached into her pocket to pull out the piece of paper from which she'd read earlier. "Do you want me to read the rest?"

Death waved an impatient hand, an indulgent hand, certain it wouldn't matter. That there would only be more talk of endings, more of life's cruelties, more loss and loss and loss, more to prove to her that humans drew the short end of the stick with their existence.

She cleared her throat and read:

And isn't it cruel,
that we only get to live it once.
Cruel, and yet, I'm grateful for
the days and weeks and months,

for nothing would be as cruel as
not having a chance to see
how beautiful it truly is
when tomorrow is not guaranteed.

Silence reigned once she finished speaking. Death felt as though something had wrapped itself tighter and tighter around him as she'd spoken, and he could not loosen the binds sufficiently to respond. Not that he was sure what he would say. No, he found himself once more uncertain, although this uncertainty came with the certainty that she would not come with him.

That he could not even ask it of her.

That he wanted her, that every bone in the body he had built himself from scratch, out here in the hospital garden, yearned and hollered and hollowed beneath the want of her, but that taking her would not be saving her from life.

No, in her eyes, it would be depriving her of it.

"The beauty of life is in the lack of guarantees," she said quietly. "It's not terrible because it ends. The knowledge that it will end, and that we don't know when or how, is what makes me grateful for each day. Because that's where we get to choose our lives. We don't get to choose the beginning or the end of it, but the middle is where we get to make it magic."

He ran his hands down his face, slowly, feeling the stretch and pull of the unfamiliar skin, wondering why that door in him had opened if it was only so soon going to slam shut. Feeling it do so with a shudder that wracked him from head to toe, from here to there and everywhere, regret tracing the shudder's steps.

What a foolish thought he'd had. He should never have decided to take a wife, should never have stopped and listened to that poem, should never have come out here and talked to her. Should never have introduced uncertainty into his certain life.

His certain *existence*.

"I'm sorry, who did you say you were?" She cut into his recriminations, folding the paper back into a small square with careful creases.

"I didn't," he said, voice hoarse, dropping his hands from his face.

She seemed to realize then that the sun had fully set, that the pinks and purples and oranges had given way to an ever-darkening blue, that nobody was out there in the garden with them. She stood abruptly from the bench and took a step away from it, pulling the veil from the moment, bursting the bubble that he'd imagined had encased them from the instant he had stepped into the garden and seen her.

He let her go.

He watched her go.

"You look familiar …" she trailed off, faltering in her retreat.

He wished she would keep walking.

He wished she would stay.

"I get that a lot," he said, forcing a smile that he hoped the shadows would mask enough for her to believe that it was real. Of course, Death would be familiar to her, so soon after she'd seen it take her grandfather. Death was familiar to everyone who had encountered it.

"Well, I should go," she said, reaching up with adept hands to pull her hair back into its original state, how it had been before it had fallen and everything else had fallen with it. "But … thank you for the conversation. It reminded me to look for the beauty in the world, while I grieve my grandfather's loss."

He nodded wordlessly. Perhaps later he would be glad to have given her that much.

"I hope you get to experience happiness," she said, pulling her car keys out of her purse, another step closer to going, to gone. "Even if it doesn't last. It's worth it. Trust me."

She turned to go, then. Death watched her until she became nothing more than a shadow, and then until her shadow blended with the other shadows, and then he just kept watching, even though there was nothing left of her to watch.

He thought that maybe, for a second there, in a door opening, in the gust that had come in through it, that had if not moved him, then shifted him—he thought that maybe, in all of that, he had experienced happiness.

And so, he kept watching as it went.

And he thought about whether it had been worth it, to have had her here beside him for so short of a time, to have heard her laugh and to have swam in the ocean of her eyes. To have imagined her beside him through the rest of eternity. To have imagined that it would be possible.

He stood up from the bench at last, late for hundreds, by now probably thousands, of appointments.

It was too soon to say yes, but Death thought perhaps it would be yes later, when enough time had passed that the door's slamming did not echo through him.

He thought perhaps yes, that it was worth it to have lost her, when for a moment, he thought he might have loved her.

Takpe

Anna Tan

Pontianak, mati beranak,
Mati ditimpa tanah tambah!
Kerat buluh panjang pendek
'Kan pelemang hati Jin Pontianak.
Dengan berkat la-ilaha ill-Allah.

Pontianak, dead in childbirth
Struck in death by earth, more earth
Cut the bamboo, long and short
Make *lemang* of the Pontianak Djinn's liver.
By the grace of the Almighty, no god but God.

There is a nail in the back of Nur's neck. She doesn't know why.

She doesn't think about it often, though sometimes when she bathes, her fingers touch it and she shudders. She doesn't pull it out; she can't, she's not allowed to. Her husband Bakri doesn't talk about it, changing the topic whenever she brings it up. She doesn't anymore.

She wants to please him.

No one else she knows has a nail there. She'd seen a girl before, on that one trip to Kuala Lumpur for her daughter, Alia's, medical check-up, a *mat salleh* with short purple hair and two little metal balls at the nape of her neck. The *mat salleh* had a lot of other metal pieces all over her body, so Nur doesn't think it's the same. Nur has looked carefully at all the other women in her kampung, her village. Most of them keep their hair in buns, under scarves, out of their faces. She leaves hers down, black and silky, reaching to the curve of her back. Bakri doesn't like her to cut it, so she doesn't.

Bakri comes in the front door, kicking off his shoes, and stooping to scoop Alia up. "And how has my little Alia been all day?"

Alia wiggles and squeals as he tosses her up in the air. For a brief moment, her fine, wavy hair circles her round face like a halo, then flops down, tussled bangs across her forehead, fluffed up around the back of her head like a little button mushroom.

Bakri winces as Alia tugs at his goatee, catches the small hand to still its grasping. His smile is wide and generous, filling out the sharp contours of his sun-darkened face.

Nur smiles, getting up from the couch. "Her birthday is coming up next week, *abang*. What do you want to do?"

"Ooo, my little Alia is going to be one, huh?" Bakri perches the little girl on his hip as he steps closer to Nur into the living room. Three steps to the right, and he would bump into their dining table. She's not sure why she keeps this distinction in her mind when it's all one cozy room. She lifts his leathery hand to her forehead, brings it to her lips.

He is all that fills her soul.

When he pulls away, she notices the sadness in his dark brown eyes he always gets when looking at her. Why, she wants to ask, but doesn't. He never tells her, only shakes his head, saying, *takpe. It's nothing.*

"Should we have a party, *abang*? Invite everyone from the kampung?" she asks. Birthdays are meant to be village-wide celebrations, a matter of pride—she knows this much. He keeps apart for her sake, but for this, for Alia, maybe he would want to do it right.

"Let's keep it small, eh, Nur? No need to call everyone."

She nods, making a mental list of their close friends. The neighbors on their left, Pak Ali and his wife Timah, but not the ones on the right; they don't like Nur. The Penghulu, definitely—the village chief would feel slighted if he and his family weren't invited. The two little girls Alia plays with and their families …

"Nur, is dinner ready?" Bakri asks, pulling her out of her thoughts.

"Ya, *abang*. Sorry!" She puts her thoughts aside and heads into the kitchen. Everything is prepared. She left them in the pots to keep warm and all she needs to do now is serve them.

Tonight, there is *kari ikan*, with more ladyfingers than fish, and *nasi putih*, the rice steamed and fluffy. Nur wishes there were more dishes, but it's all they can afford. If they slaughter a chicken, tomorrow they might have meat, but then what would they do for eggs in the future? The banana trees in the back make up for it. She finds them comforting. Alia loves them as a snack, whether fresh or fried in batter. Bakri—he turns away from the fruit, looking sick. Although she remembers, somehow, that he used to love *pisang goreng*, loved it fresh and dripping with oil, the batter they'd been dipped in a recipe handed down from her grandmother. She remembers that, although she cannot remember anything else, not since the incident.

"What's wrong, *sayang*?" Bakri stops eating, fingers smeared with curry.

She shakes her head. "*Takpe.*"

The phrase passes between them so often it too means nothing: *Takpe. Takde ape-pe.* Doesn't matter. It's nothing. Never mind. It's fine.

They talk about birthday parties instead.

The party is planned for Saturday, the day before Alia's birthday. The anniversary of the incident that wiped out all of Nur's memories. Not to say that she remembers Alia's birth. She just remembers the pain of it, living in its haze, until the local bomoh had taken the pain away. They'd moved after that, Bakri packing them up in the middle of the night and sneaking them into an abandoned house on the edge of a forest. They'd only moved to this village six months ago. The Penghulu is a sweet man who doesn't speak much. Bakri prefers it that way.

Nur chops onions while Timah gossips beside her, seated on the long bench just outside the back door. There's shade from the awning, enough to keep the burning sun off them. The slight breeze is sticky-cool. The long, wooden table is weathered and sagging due to age, not the scattered foodstuff and spices they've gathered for tomorrow. Timah's bulk is motherly, comforting, her thighs the sought-after pillow for grumpy children to nestle in. She has a thick neck and a wobbly triple chin, as well as a warbly voice her grandchildren can hear from the other end of the village.

It feels familiar in some ways, like something she used to do. It's not quite a feast they're making, but close. Bakri will be happy. Between the two of them, Nur and Timah, they're cooking for Nur's family and thirteen guests, but with more than enough for anyone else who drops by. Just the way it's supposed to be done, even if Bakri doesn't acknowledge it. It's jarring, because he used to be quite easy-going, hospitable. Nur doesn't know what has changed. It's just one of the things they've stopped talking about.

"Eh, Nur, so when are you trying for the next one?" Timah's question breaks through her thoughts.

"Next one?"

"*Ya lah*, one enough meh?"

Nur feels her cheeks heating up. She shrugs.

"Bakri doesn't want, is it?"

Nur shrugs again.

"Don't need to be so shy, it's just the two of us."

But Nur doesn't know what to say. She doesn't know how to explain the strange distance between them, the sorrow in Bakri's eyes, how he's changed. How can she, when she cannot remember exactly how he used to be?

"Anyway, have you met the new family?"

"New family?" Nur asks, grateful that Timah has changed the subject.

"They arrived yesterday, Muhammad and Khadijah, my Ali says. Funny, isn't it! Just like the prophet!"

Nur smiles, a stirring of unease in her liver. The names sound familiar, though they're common enough. "Family, you said?"

"Yes, with two little boys. Twins! Oooh, so *comel!* They make me want to squeeze their cheeks."

"Cuter than Alia then."

Timah laughs, a hearty, bellyful sound. "Don't you know, *sayang*, no child's cheeks are safe from me."

Nur hates it when Timah calls her *sayang*, as if Nur were her child. The endearment, Nur feels, should be kept for true family, true lovers, like the way Bakri claims her again and again when he names her so, even through his tears. She doesn't tell Timah this. *Takpe*, she will endure for the sake of their friendship. "Where are they from?"

Timah is about to answer when Bakri runs into view and skids to a stop in front of them, body tense and dripping with sweat.

"We have to go."

Nur's hand tightens around the knife in fear, mouth gaping before she manages to say, "Where, *abang*?" What about the party?

"What's wrong, Bakri?" Timah interrupts.

"*Takde ape-pe*," he replies flippantly. "We have to go, Nur. *Now*. Get Alia."

She goes, leaving Timah amidst a table of chopped onions and crushed garlic, curry leaves and coriander, the coconut milk curdling because they've forgotten it's there.

It's three days before they stop running through tall trees and thick underbrush, before they find a place that Bakri feels safe enough to stay. She slaps at the mosquitoes that swarm them, holding Alia close to her chest. The trees have thinned here, though the *lalang*, the tall grasses they wade through, comes up to the middle of Nur's leg. Burrs cling to her clothes, makes her feet itch. Someone must have lived here a long time ago. Nur sees banana trees clustered at the other end of the clearing.

"What's going on, *abang*?" Nur asks, but Bakri doesn't answer. He just looks at her sadly and a little fearfully.

"*Takde ape-pe.*"

But it's not nothing, not with Alia hungry and hot and frightened.

"*Abang*, tell me." It's the first time Nur insists on anything, and the fear she holds in her heart is written on her husband's face. She scratches at her neck, lifts her hair from where it's annoying her, thick, heavy, and slick with sweat.

He stumbles over his words as he scrambles backwards away from her. "They can't see you."

"Me?" She stutters to a stop, hands around her child.

"*Takpe, takde ape-pe,*" he mumbles, reaching out for Alia.

It doesn't placate Nur this time, although she lets him take the girl. "Why?"

Evening is falling and it's growing dim in the small clearing. Nur finds a stump to sit on, near to the banana trees. Bakri stays at the other end of the clearing, gripping Alia so tightly she whines.

"Muhammad and Khadijah were from our old kampung."

Nur cocks her head to one side, trying to understand. "What happened in our old kampung?" *It's the key,* she thinks. The incident Bakri never talks about is the key to everything.

Bakri shakes his head, obstinate.

She clicks her tongue in frustration. "We can't just keep running away."

"We must."

"What kind life will this be for Alia?"

"You can't ... I can't just ..."

She waits, but Bakri doesn't continue, slumping back against a tree instead, letting tears fall. He cries too much, too often now. He releases his grip on Alia and the girl crawls towards Nur. Nur tracks her progress by the rustling of the *lalang*.

"Do you love me?" Bakri asks finally.

Nur swipes at the sweat accumulating around her neck, tosses her head. Her hair snags on something as she tries to lift it so she gives it a quick tug. Something shifts. The smell of frangipani fills the air. She looks around, trying to find its source.

Bakri freezes.

"Alia! Alia come here." His voice is shrill.

"What's going on, Bakri?" Nur asks. She doesn't feel the urge to call him *abang* anymore, doesn't feel the connection that makes him her husband.

"Nur, what is there at the back of your neck?"

The question makes her pause. She reaches underneath her hair and touches the place where the nail used to be. It is no longer there. "*Takde ape-pe.*"

Bakri scrambles for his daughter before she gets to Nur. "Alia! Come, Alia! Come to *ayah*."

Alia sits, looking between Nur and Bakri, confused.

Nur feels like she's unstoppered, watching the color leach out of her body, her nails lengthening. All that she is, has been, is spilling out of the hole in her neck. She flexes claw-like fingers, tongue brushing the sharpening edges of her teeth. Her eyes glow red.

"I'm sorry," Bakri mutters under his breath over and over again.

It's dark in the forest now and the man is a brown lump on the floor, hugging a little girl. Nur floats over to them. She's hungry. He is male, prey, helpless. She needs to feed.

"I couldn't—I didn't want to lose you. You died, and I—I'm sorry!" His voice is a wail, but he doesn't look up, holding the girl close to him. Shielding her eyes, blocking her nose.

Frangipanis and rot. Sweet and pungent. Nur looks down at herself, at the blood-smeared white dress she doesn't remember putting on. She doesn't remember anything, other than pain, other than dying. Why is she here if she's dead? What unfinished business does she have that she's a pontianak? A deadly, vampiric Djinn?

"She's yours, Alia is yours. Please, don't harm us. I just needed you for longer, I couldn't let you go."

The pontianak doesn't know where she is. She is far from her burial grounds, far from home. She is lost, and hunger gnaws, fresh blood calling to her. But this man, this child, are familiar, though she doesn't know why. Is she meant to revenge herself on him?

The man is scrambling in the ground, as if he's found something. She bends to see what he's holding. He's muttering under his breath and though she cannot hear the words, the tone of it frightens her. She shies away from them, then stops as the child holds out a hand to her. The pontianak stares, mesmerized. She reaches out to touch that thin, brown hand.

The man shifts the child in his arms, snatching her away again. "Don't harm her, Nur. She's yours. You took care of her for a whole year, remember?" He gulps, turns so the child is facing her. "Alia, remember Alia?"

The pontianak ignores him, smiling at the child. Why would she harm the girl? Warmth fills her. She misses the babe in her belly, the one she longs to hold in her arms, the one she's stayed to take care of.

"That's good, Nur. Good, Alia. Let her hold you, let *ibu* hold you one more time."

There is movement behind her, but the pontianak sees it too late. A sharp pain drills into the back of her neck.

She screams.

When Nur awakes, the world is too bright, too sharp. It wobbles until she holds a hand out, touches Bakri beside her.

"Where are we?" She croaks, looking around the unfamiliar hut. Bright sun peeks through the cracks in the walls, moss-covered planks that have warped and no longer fit together properly. The roof sags.

"Almost home, Nur. Almost home."

"Did something happen?" She feels as if she's lost time. "Did I fall sick? I'm sorry."

Bakri's face is lined with worry. "*Takpe. Takde apa-apa.*"

"Where's Alia?"

"Sleeping." He moves, and when Nur props herself up on an elbow, she sees the small form of her daughter curled around a pillow nearby.

Bakri helps her sit up, then sits beside her, a hand caressing her neck, pressing against the nail. He looks rumpled, crumpled.

"Are you okay?" Nur asks.

"No, but *takpe*. I'll be fine."

He packs up silently. Nur comes alongside to help, but he shrugs, saying he's got it. He does. They leave the hut.

She sits holding Alia on the buffalo cart. "Where did you get this?"

"Bought it from a nearby kampung." Bakri's eyes flit between the muddy track they're travelling on and Nur. It's a straight road with no turnoffs, but he doesn't want to stare at her.

She watches the mud churn under the wheels, like her thoughts spinning with half-formed questions. "Must have been expensive. I'm sorry."

"*Takpe. Takde apa-apa.*"

Nur looks out at the paddy fields. They've left the rainforest behind. "Timah will be glad to see us."

"We're not going back there," Bakri says.

"You said we were going home." Her eyes narrow at the vaguely familiar scenery. One paddy field looks like another, she supposes.

Bakri makes a weird sound in the back of his throat. "Home, Nur. To our old kampung. To before."

"Oh." She blinks, trying to process. Bakri has never wanted to talk about that place. "How long until we get there?"

"Soon. Tonight, most probably."

It's dusk when they approach the village. A strange sense of familiarity creeps over Nur. She's not sure if it's because she truly recognizes the place, or because it looks just like the one they've left. Graceful wooden houses sit on stilts next to squat white-washed brick-and-cement monstrosities. The call of the Azan fades in the distance. It's quiet, save for the soft clucks of chickens roosting. Everyone has gone home for dinner.

Bakri skirts the cluster of houses, causing Nur to look askance at him.

"Trust me," he says when he notices her gaze.

"Who are you avoiding?"

"No one." He fidgets.

They pull to a stop at the graveyard. It's on a grassy patch of land outside the village, filled with tight rows of small, knobbly headstones, all facing Mecca. Dry leaves flutter in the soft breeze. There is the wet, earthy smell of freshly-turned soil.

Nur frowns at her husband. "*Abang*, what are you not telling me?"

"I'm sorry, Nur, for everything." He glances over his shoulder, looking for someone.

"What?" Something feels wrong.

Bakri helps her down from the cart, his hands trembling. When he next speaks, his voice is heavy, rough. "*Sayang*, I'm laying you to rest. Like I should have a year ago."

"*Abang*?" Her voice squeaks with fear.

An older man approaches them. His face is wrinkled, grey hair tucked under a black songkok. There is earth clinging to his clothes, but his hands are scrubbed clean. Nur recognizes the bomoh.

"You got my message then," Bakri says, wiping his hands down the sides of his pants.

"I told you nothing good would come of this."

"Bakri?" Nur shakes where she stands.

The man has been digging up a grave. *Her* grave. Her body shudders. She feels the call of home tugging against her sense of unfinished business.

She cannot go, not yet.

Bakri looks down at his feet, then turns to Alia. "Come, *sayang*. Come to *ayah*."

Nur's throat is dry, her voice hoarse. "Why?"

The bomoh takes Nur by the hand and the back of her neck, around the nail, compelling her to lie down.

"*Abang?*"

"Shh, Nur. I thought that I could have you, that it was my right to keep you."

Nur doesn't struggle, still under Bakri's power. Her connection to him is still strong, her knowledge that he is her husband, her world, eclipsing her terror of the bomoh. The bomoh puts an egg under each of her armpits, places needles in the palms of her hands. She lays very still, fixing her eyes on Bakri's face. The bomoh wraps her in a white shroud, tying ropes around her body so she cannot move. Numbness starts to creep over her as they lift her into the coffin.

"I'm sorry I did this to you, that I allowed this to happen to you. You should have gone in peace, gone to rest." He swallows hard, clears his throat. "But I wanted Alia to know you too. Can you forgive me?"

There are tears in Bakri's eyes.

"*Takpe. Takde ape-pe.*" There is nothing to forgive. It's the last thing Nur says as the bomoh puts glass beads in her mouth and lifts her head gently to pull out the nail.

The fragrance of frangipanis fills the air, fingernails struggle to lengthen, a sharp hunger consuming her, eyes flashing red as they fix on that man, *she should know who he is*, but she is held in place by the charms as much as by Bakri's love. Consciousness fades as first the light goes, a veil placed over her head, the coffin lid strapped tight. Then sound fades. There is only the soft thudding of earth as they bury her again, this time for good.

Bakri weeps over Nur's grave, Alia in his arms.

Loss seems worse, the second time round.

Uber For the Undead

H. A. Titus

It's not every night that you come face to face with the undead. Then again, I'm not your normal Uber driver either.

… Maybe I should back up.

My name is Benji. Benjamin Harding, if you want to get formal about it. The first undead I ever picked up was a ghost, only I didn't realize it until afterward. You know that whole thing about cabby drivers being front-seat therapists? Well, it was true that night. The poor guy just needed someone to talk to about all of his issues. Once we got those sorted—on a long, rambling drive all over the city—he politely thanked me and dissipated, moving onward into the afterlife, nearly taking me with him. Stiffed me on the fare though.

Ghosts can be jerks.

Since then, I've picked up ghosts, zombies, draugr, liches, ghouls, and vampires. All of them have their downsides—the first lich I ever drove anywhere tried to ensorcell me into being his cabby forever, and zombies sometimes shed bits of skin and organs, so clean-up can be a mess—but over the last five years, I've gotten used to it.

The only repeat client I've ever had, though, is Delilah.

Delilah Crow, specifically. Although I'm not sure if that's an alias, or her real name. Seems awfully fitting for a vampire. I once wondered out loud to her about never meeting a vampire with a name like Fred, or George, or Humphrey. It made her laugh. Despite being an undead, she has a pretty laugh.

Delilah had been turned back in the nineteen-fifties and still had this bright, red-and-polka-dots, rockabilly thing going on. Big red curls on the top of her head, swingy skirts, red lips, that kind of look. Chatty, for a vampire. Delilah was the one who taught me about the undead—well, except vampires. I'd been able to drag a few facts out of her, but mostly, she didn't talk about her own kind.

Usually, it's only once a week or so that she calls up and asks for me. So when her number pops up on my phone on a Friday, after I'd just talked to her on a Tuesday, I am a bit surprised.

I pull to the curb in front of her apartment building and wait. After a few minutes, I roll my window down. There's a bit of a wind tonight, and the threat of rain. It makes the city smell fresh and clean rather than stale and full of garbage.

Delilah swings out of the front door of her building. Tonight, she's dressed in a long, shapeless black coat that nearly reaches the ground. Her red hair is pulled back in a braid and tucked under a stocking cap.

She gets into the passenger seat and smiles at me. "Hey, Benji. How's your sister? Did she have her baby yet?"

"Hey, Del." I smile back. "Yeah, she had another girl. That makes Caleb and Jeremy outnumbered now." I put the car into gear and pull back onto the street. "You're in a good mood tonight."

"Yeah, what makes you say that?"

I gesture to my mouth. "No fangs." I'd only seen her shiny, snake-like fangs twice—once, when she showed me, and once, when she'd gotten angry.

Delilah presses her lips together, trying to hide her smile, and looks down at her lap. "Well, let's hope it stays that way, okay?"

The comment hangs in the air, an uncomfortable silence between us. There's a weird energy around her tonight. She reminds me more of the other vampires I'd met. The ones who like to hide under wide-brimmed hats and tall collars.

I clear my throat and turn the wheel, beginning our usual route. Delilah once told me that she'd always enjoyed riding in taxis back before she was turned. "You always met such interesting drivers then," she says.

Delilah leans into her seat corner, crosses her legs, and drums her fingers on her knee. She doesn't look at me, but I can see her reflection in the window. Thanks to modern makeup, she looks tanned and healthy, if a bit thin, with sharp cheekbones. Tonight, she has dark purple eyeshadow and no lipstick. Another deviation from the usual.

I reach down and turn on my phone, selecting my favorite playlist: a mix of classic rock that spanned the fifties, sixties, and seventies. I'd tailored it especially for these once-a-week midnight drives.

Delilah smiles when the first strains of "Jailhouse Rock" filter through the speakers. But it's a small, sad smile that only touches the corners of her lips.

I start to ask what's wrong, but she shakes her head. "Don't worry about it, Benji. I'm just in a mood tonight."

We drive without talking, long enough for the playlist to cycle through several songs.

Delilah suddenly sits up, eyes narrowing. As I slow for a red light, I glance out her window. We're passing a park, and sitting on the rock wall around the playground are two girls, laughing as they look at their phones, the bright screens making their faces glow white.

Delilah taps the window, and I spot something I missed at first glance—the darker black-on-black, shadow-in-a-shadow behind the girls, on the other side of the playground.

"Pull over here," Delilah orders me.

"Del—"

"Don't 'Del' me," she snaps. "Just do it, Benji."

I sigh, pull through the now-green light, and find a parallel space across the street from the park. She'd never told me, but I guessed a while ago that this was how she'd been turned—a surprise attack at night, when she was walking through the city alone. Every time she sees teenage girls out on their own at night, she gets upset. Sometimes, she does this. She sees the stalkers and the lurkers, and she makes sure they know someone's watching. Someone who will take them out if they try to hurt innocent kids.

Before I even fully put the car in park, Delilah is out the door.

It swings shut silently behind her—something else I chalk up to her vampiric powers, because honestly, who ever heard of a car door being quiet on its own?

I swear under my breath. This is new. I can't spot her in the shadows. Like the other creeping monsters of the night, she melds into the darkness perfectly.

I sigh and lean back in my seat. I should be used to it by now. At first, I'd wondered why Delilah always wanted me to drive through the old, crumbling center of the city. At least twice a night—sometimes three or four times—we'd pull over, and she'd roll down the window and stare out at … something. And she'd always warn me to look away.

At first I thought it was because she didn't want me to see. After a few weeks, I realized it was because she didn't want *them* to see *me*. To see my face. And I'd started listening to her—because the last thing I wanted was the supernatural mafia to know my face.

But she'd never gotten out of the car before.

So tonight, I watch.

The teen girls on their phones don't even flinch, don't even notice something is happening behind them. One minute, the darkened blot of the stalker is there, and the next, it's gone.

The darkness seems to press around my car, and I feel as though eyes are on me. Watching. My own lurkers in the dark. The hair prickles on my neck and arms. I glance over my shoulder, out my window, but there's nothing out there.

I turn back.

Delilah appears in the passenger window, skin pale against the dark sky.

I jump, fold forward, and let out a gasping laugh. "You scared me."

She climbs back into the passenger seat. Leaning back, she takes a deep breath and I can see her fangs, glittering with blood. The prickling sensation on my arms returns.

Blood. She's killed whatever the stalker was. I draw in a breath. Sometimes, it's easy to forget that my friend is a vampire. A mon—*no*. I shove the thought away. Not a monster.

She sees me looking and closes her mouth. Clicks her tongue against the roof of her mouth to retract the fangs.

I face forward and dig my fingers into the leather of my steering wheel. The first time I'd seen her fangs, she'd only clicked them out as a warning to a stubborn lurker. That one had challenged her, stepping out into the moonlight so even my human eyes could see the lump that suggested a nose, the dents for eyes, and the stretching, gaping maw of a mouth. Delilah had hissed and shown her fangs, and the faceless, nameless thing had cowered and crept away.

But the blood tonight? I swallow hard. Close my eyes. My stomach wobbles.

What has she done? I reach down, put my hand on the console between us. My jacket is draped over it. I can see the bulge in the pocket, the flask of holy water I've kept there since she'd admitted it was a real vampire deterrent. Inside the console are other monster deterrents. Bags of grains and rice to distract. At one point I'd kept garlic in there, but the smell became overwhelming. I don't think crucifixes do anything, but I have one hanging on my rearview mirror anyway.

They were not for her. They were for other vamps. Other monsters.

Because I've never truly thought of Delilah as a monster.

"Better drive, Benji," she says quietly.

I pull back into the street. After spending a few minutes calming myself, taking deep breaths and reminding myself that Delilah has never, ever been a threat to me, I say, "So was it a creeper?" I try to sound casual even though my stomach is still twisting.

"They're always creepers."

I hesitate. "I saw blood. Did you—"

"Watch it. You keep getting nosy and I'll just turn into a bat and flutter right out this window," she warns.

Her tone is deadpan, but out of the corner of my eye I can see the smile tugging the corners of her lips. Back to business as usual. I should smile at the familiar joke, but tonight, the thought of her leaving me makes my skin go cold.

She's not a monster, she's not a monster, I repeat to myself, but tonight she's skirting the edge more than she's ever had before. What if I'm the only thing keeping her from that edge? I want to stop, pull to the side of the road, and ask her what's wrong.

"Turning into a bat doesn't solve life problems, Del," I say instead. My usual reply to the joke. Maybe this is the way I can help tonight. Keeping things as normal as possible.

"Oh, I know, but it's awfully fun anyway."

The strains of "Blue Suede Shoes" fills the car.

"So is it a real vampiric power?" I ask quietly.

Delilah shifts in her seat. "The bat part?"

"Yeah."

She smirks. "How do you know any of the vampire stuff? I don't meet many normals who do, and I haven't told you that much."

"Yeah, wouldn't want to violate the vampire code," I joke. Then I shrug. "There are the legends, obviously, and confirmation of them out there on the internet, if you know where to look. And if you're okay with digging through the weird stuff."

She arches a delicate eyebrow. "The weird stuff, huh?"

"You know what I mean," I say back. Just like that, the tension eases a bit.

It's strange to say your best friend is a vampire, but in my case, it is kind of true.

And yet, not true at all. I barely know anything about Delilah. Not like friends should. Sure, I know her favorite place to get fried fish and chips—which she still ate even though it upset her stomach—and that she has a black cat named Dracula.

And that she likes to ride through the streets at night, warning off creeps who stalk teenagers. Not just teen girls. We stopped when we saw teen boys being followed. But usually, it was the girls.

We drive for a bit, the streetlights running yellow and black stripes over us.

"I found the ones who turned me," Delilah says suddenly, her voice tight and tense.

I tighten my hands on the wheel.

She glances at me out of the corners of her eyes. "You okay?"

"Yeah, I just ... I thought we were done talking tonight."

"Do I often do that?"

Shut down after scaring off a creeper? Yes. I risk a quick glance over to her. She's staring at me, eyes glimmering, looking strangely intense. I settle for a shrug. "You were saying?"

She turns back to the window, tucks one foot up on the seat, and wraps her arms around her knee. I can see now that underneath the long black coat, she's wearing tight, black clothing. I frown. That's far outside of Delilah's usual style. What was going on?

I'm just starting to think she's done talking after all when her voice, small and quiet and very un-Delilah-like, reaches my ears. I reach down and turn off the music.

"The ones who turned me. My sires. I've been searching for them ever since 1958." Delilah bites her lower lip. "I was eighteen. Walking home by myself, late at night, after a party at a friend's house. My boyfriend and I'd had a fight. I thought I was walking in an all right part of town, but ... I was jumped when I was walking past an alley." Her voice pinches off and her face wrinkles like she might cry.

Can vampires cry?

I pop open my center console and hand her a box of tissues.

She gives me a wobbly smile and takes the box.

"So what happened?" I ask.

She shrugs. "I woke up the next morning, shaken awake by a police officer. I ... bit him, before I realized what I was doing. Not enough to turn him, I later found out, but enough to give me strength to run. And I ran." She gives a strained laugh. "I spent the first forty years running. I was scared of myself. Every time I tried to feed, I ended up vomiting. Most vampires believe that you take what you need, by force. I've met a few who believe you can ask, that we can create a symbiotic relationship between vampire and human. But no matter what, feeding from humans made me sick. I thought I was disgusting."

"You're *not* disgusting." The heat of my words surprises me. I flex my stinging hand, as if I could work out the burning in my chest. That twisting mess of anger and fear that makes me hot and cold at the same time.

"I'm better about it now," she says. "It helps that I subsist on animal blood. It's not quite as good, but with that and vitamins, I get by."

"Does it affect your powers at all?" I ask. Because I can't not ask.

She laughs, raises her eyebrows. "Powers?" There's a slight teasing lilt to her voice, but underneath it I can still hear her tension. Her anger.

"Maybe that's dramatic," I admit.

"Maybe a little. And I don't know. I've never noticed that much of a difference, but I also switched to animal blood pretty quickly." She taps the windowsill. "Anyway, I've been trying to find my sires." Her face darkens. "They didn't care. They drank and left me, abandoned me. I nearly starved to death multiple times before I found other vampires who could take me in, teach me how to cope."

Something dawns on me, and this time I blurt it out before I can think better of it. "Your midnight drives. This has been practice, hasn't it?"

She doesn't answer.

I pull to the curb hard and park the car. My hands start shaking again. I look around the outside of the car. I've been following our usual route without thinking about it, and we're in the factory district. I drop my hands from the wheel and start jiggling my leg.

"What're you going to do when you find them?"

More silence.

I get the feeling that I should just leave it here. The knot in the center of my gut tightens. I shouldn't push any more. I should just keep driving, and maybe next week, we can pretend that this never happened. That it can go back to normal—whatever 'normal' was for a guy who drove around his vampire friend once a week.

But I know our "normal" is over now.

"Delilah?" I look over.

She's staring straight ahead, her mouth set in hard lines, her eyes glowing with the thrill of the hunt.

"No, no, no." I shake my head. "Delilah, I can't. I can't be a party to this." I never wanted to get on the supernatural radar. So far, it had only been the occasional drive. Then Delilah every week. But even then, I'd made an effort not to be seen. Not to get involved.

"They deserve it," she snaps.

"Del—"

"No!" She shouts and swivels her head to glare at me. Her movements are too fast. Her glare too intense, her eyes fever bright. She opens her mouth, and her fangs click down into place, ready to bite.

I swear and press my back against the door, heart thundering in my chest as I fumble for the latch. I wrench the door open and fall out of the car. My elbows scrape against the pavement, and my breath is knocked out of my lungs. I scramble to my feet.

Delilah pops open her door and stands, holding out one hand. "Benji, stop!"

I take a step backward. Would she kill me outright or turn me?

Delilah's nostrils flare. She reaches back into the car, grabs my jacket, and tosses it over the roof of the car to me.

"Cover that." She points to my elbow.

I look down and see blood and loose skin smeared across the back of my arm. I pull on the jacket and rub at the stinging wound through the soft sweatshirt material.

"And here, if it makes you feel better."

I look up as she lobs the flask of holy water at me. I catch it, clutch it to my chest.

"Benji," Delilah pleads. "Have I ever done anything to harm you? Ever tried to charm you, even? You know what vampires can do. Think about it—have I ever once used my *powers* on you?"

Vampires were swift, cunning, charming. I know that. And I know that if she had me charmed, I wouldn't be outside my car right now, shaking with adrenaline, my hands gripping the cold flask of holy water. I'd been charmed, once, by a vampire who had just wanted a free ride. I remember the panic of being trapped in my own mind, unable to control my own actions.

And that vampire had never shown up again after Delilah had a 'talk' with him. A cold sweat broke out on my neck and back. She'd probably killed him. Just like she'd killed the lurker tonight.

"I don't want to be this way, Benji," Delilah says, her voice pleading. "But I wasn't given a choice. And the ones who turned me? They won't show any restraint. They haven't—I've checked. They've turned others, unwillingly. Just six months ago I met a guy who was turned by one of them—he's barely getting by. He looks like a walking skeleton. Not everyone is lucky. And despite what you've been told, yes, vampires can die. Not from old age. But being starved to death, or unable to get enough nutrients from the blood we drink? That's a reality. And more importantly, they can be killed."

"So you're going to kill them," I say flatly.

She nods.

"Okay," I say. "But I can't drive you there. Whatever you do, Delilah, there will be an investigation—if not by the police, then by other vampires. I don't want people finding out I was involved. I have a sister, Del." I'm the one pleading now. "I have a niece and a nephew. I can't risk it. I don't want to get involved in the supernatural mafia. It was fine when you were just scaring off creeps, but now ..."

I trail off. I'm not sure what else I can say. If there *is* anything else to say.

Slowly, she nods. "Of- of course. I'm sorry, Benji." She sounds genuine. "I'm sorry for scaring you. That wasn't my intention. And you're righ—this isn't your vendetta. It isn't fair to ask you to become this involved."

I watch as Delilah reaches inside the car, grabs her bag, slings it over her shoulder. She turns and begins walking away.

"Del?" I call.

She turns and looks over her shoulder.

"See you next week?"

She smiles a sad smile that makes tear-drop shapes of her eyes, and turns the corner.

I sit down on the curb and clasp my hands together. I'm still shaking. The stoplight down the street clicks, turning green.

Another soft click, more fleshy, less metallic, sounds behind me.

The hair on the back of my neck stands upright. I spin, going for the flask in my pocket.

A blur of motion hits me in the chest, throws me against the hood of the car. Curved fangs flash in the streetlights, shiny and yellow.

Vampire.

I yell in panic and block my throat with my arm. The smooth flask slips from my fingers and clangs on the pavement. A face looms over me—male, fangs and teeth slick with drool, the eyes alight with the dark thrill of the hunt that I'd just seen in Delilah's eyes.

The vampire's fangs sink into my arm and I scream, kicking at him. He wrenches his head, tearing my skin and throwing me to the ground. My shoulder crunches into the sidewalk, sending a flare of pain into my back. I look up. My flask lays on its side, the stopper still in place. I scrabble forward, grab it, roll onto my back just as the vampire grabs me again.

I pop the flask's lid and throw it into the vampire's face.

The creature jerks away, his shriek splitting the night. I stand up, panting, and watch as the vampire claws at his face and chest. The holy water bubbles like acid, eating into the pale skin. The vampire snarls at me, eyes slitted in hatred—and then it turns, galloping away through the night. Vanishing around the corner after Delilah.

Delilah.

I snatch the empty flask from the ground, throw open my car door. Leaning in, I grab the keys from the ignition and dig into the console. I find the fist-sized bag of grain and the back-up flask of holy water, then grab the small crucifix hanging from the rearview mirror and run after the vampire.

My lungs ache. It feels like I'm already getting bruises from the vampire slamming me against my car. The black and yellow stripes of streetlights flicker overhead. I can just keep the monster in sight as it lopes through the back streets and alleyways. It's eerie, silent. All the normal noises of the city—the car horns, the screech of tires, the dogs barking, the whistle of wind through the buildings—sound far away. The air is thick and humid and makes breathing hard.

I break out of the maze of back streets and find myself in a plaza. The white, clean concrete almost sparkles in the moonlight, and the trees planted here and there among the stone benches provide shadows. Too many shadows. Anything could be hiding there, waiting for me.

The vampire I was following limps into the building on the far side of the plaza. It's a smaller building, only a few stories tall and planed in shiny, reflective windows. I can see my reflection—I look very small, my lanky frame shortened, my dark eyes just holes in my colorless face, distorted in the glass. As I step forward, my image wavers, matching the feeling in my chest.

I stand there, clutching the crucifix and the bag of grain and the flask, and feel like an idiot. Like I'm trying to be a vampire hunter in the TV shows—only I'm the stupid one, the newbie who gets eaten in the first five minutes of the show to give the experts a mystery to solve. That's my role here. That's the part I'm going to play.

I shake my head and step forward again.

An ear-splitting *boom* shatters the air. The ground shakes under my feet, and I stagger down to my knees. When I look up, I see the reflective windows of the building blown halfway across the plaza, scattered like stars in a galaxy. Red bursts of flame licking out of gaping holes in the building's sides.

"Delilah!" I shout, even though I know it's useless. Something stings my eye and I wipe at my face. The back of my hand comes away red. I touch my forehead and realize some of the shards of glass must've made it further than I thought. I'm bleeding.

"Delilah!" I yell again.

My only answer is the crackle of fire. Even across the plaza I can feel the searing heat. The way the flames crack my skin, suck out the moisture. I squint against the blazing yellow and white light. Nothing moves inside the building except for the devouring flames. I lean forward, suddenly weak and sick, and rest my elbows on my knees. I'm trembling all over.

If Delilah was in that building with the other vampires, she won't have survived. No one could've survived.

"Del." My voice cracks, and I press my hands against my mouth. Somewhere in the distance, sirens wail.

The sound makes me jerk upright. I can't be seen here. Ashes from the fire begin to patter on the ground, coating the bright white concrete with splotches of gray.

I limp back to my car in a daze. Hang the crucifix back over my mirror. Drop the bag of grains and the extra flask on the passenger seat. That's when I see it—the white envelope, with my name neatly lettered on the outside.

To Benji, my dearest friend.

"I hope you're at peace, Del." I choke the words out. Then I turn the key, put the car into gear, and drive away.

I walk down the path of the little rundown house at the edge of the bad part of town. It's been a month since the explosion. The cut has mostly healed into a scar that neatly bisects my right eyebrow.

In my jacket pocket, I carry the letter from Delilah. The one where she told me what a saving grace our rides together had been. How important our friendship had been to her. But how it had been time to stop hiding. To stop others from being hurt as she had been.

My fear was still there, along with a healthy new dose of respect for vampires. But it felt good to know that she'd considered us friends, and that it hadn't just been me.

In my hand, I carry a plastic bag that's heavily weighed down. I can smell the livers even through their layers of plastic packaging. I hate liver. I hate the way it smells like iron. I'd chosen the bloodiest packages I could find.

I pause in front of the door, take a deep breath, and knock.

After a few seconds, it cracks open. The moonlight glints off the golden chains—three of them—in place, keeping the door from opening too far. An eye—sunken and almost too bloodshot to tell what color it is—appears in the crack, and a thin-lipped mouth speaks.

"You should leave," he says.

"Paul, right?" I say.

"Go away."

I pushed the letter towards the door. "I have a letter from Delilah."

He freezes in the act of closing the door. "Delilah?"

"Yeah. I know she talked to you, Paul. You guys discussed your sires, among other things. She told me you'd been having a rough time."

"Delilah's dead," Paul mutters.

"I know," I say quietly. I let the plastic bag swing a bit in my hand. "Can we talk out here? I brought snacks."

Paul begins unlocking the chains on the door. "If you're Delilah's friend ... who are you?"

I smile. "I'm Benji. I'm an Uber driver, and I specialize in helping the undead."

Out of the Sea

Savannah Jezowski

I rise, out of the sea I rise,
a specter of the deep,
salt-kissed skin, seaweed hair,
and briny fish scales.
I hear the call of canvas sails
snapping wild in the wind,
the stir of oars dipping
in my bed of sea foam.
I see wild souls who do not heed
the warnings of the rocks
and plot their course across
the siren's watery realm.

I sing a song of lost dreams,
of shadows reaching
across the barren seas
to taint the crest of waves
that kiss the barnacled hulls of ships.
I tantalize their senses
on fog-cloaked seas concealed
and draw them deftly to me;
they come, fools reaching for their deaths.
So I sing a song of passion,

A Kind of Death

of steel fishhooks
and sun-bleached mermaid bones.

Gently I banish their fears,
curl my mists around their eyes,
raise the ghosts of past ships
sunken in my embrace.
Specters haunt the listing deck,
calling their brothers
to join them in my black waters
with the other skeletal ships.
I rise, out of the sea I rise
to sing a sultry song
that beckons all the sailors
to the siren's watery grave.

I sing a song of hatred,
with monsters from the deep;
my song strikes out like thunder
rolling across the waves.
I raise the ships with ghost shroud
to dance across the seas
as dry-lightning flashes
across the writhing sky.
I sing—terror fills their wild eyes
as their blood begins to freeze.
I drag the ships of sailors
to the fathoms of the deep.

I sing a song of loneliness,
the oceans still and barren,
the ships afraid to leave their moorings
and venture across my waves.
They snared my sisters,
I sank their ships,

but now what remains?
Only mermaid bones and lifeless sails
and memories of regret.
The seas are mine now.
I sink into the waves and wish
we'd chosen more than death.

The Price of Ashes

Zimri A. Z. Zoran

"You are sure about this, young man?"

"I wouldn't have come if I wasn't."

"What will you relinquish in return?"

He rolled the sack off his shoulder, hefting it onto the desk. The woman laughed. "Centuries of wealthy kings lived and died in their halls of jewels, and you think gold will buy you eternal life?"

"What do you want, then?"

The woman folded her fingers: knotted, scarred, and wrapped in fabric. "To be mortal is to be human. To be immortal is to forsake your humanity. Are you prepared for such a sacrifice?"

His gaze hardened. "What would I have to do?"

The woman's sooty eyes crinkled. She opened a dusty chest and retrieved a bottle containing dust, or maybe ash. "You are familiar with the Mount that Burns in the West?"

He nodded.

The woman smiled. "Jump into the heart of its flame."

Something inside him choked, but the rest was too far gone. Still, caution clung to the fringes of his tenacity. "How will that not destroy me?"

The woman shook the bottle of ash. "Mix it with oil and paint it on your eyes, nose, and heart. The rest you will drink."

"You are swindling me."

"Such is why immortality is a legend to the world of men. Many have come, but few have nerve enough to try."

Something inside him burned. "I require power to rule this land forever, no matter the cost! Do not compare me to the spineless!"

The woman waggled the bottle in front of him, but when he reached for it, she yanked it away. "Many have said the same, and their desires are insufficient. Now, young man, you are certain this is what you want?"

He lunged for the bottle again, and again she tore it from his grasp. The woman held up a gnarled finger and clicked at him. "Patience, now. Your humanity you give for this power that you seek, but the bottle …" She licked her crooked teeth as she eyeballed his sack of gold. "It has its own price."

With a snarl, he let her haul the riches behind her desk. He snatched the bottle, but the woman clutched his wrist before he could pocket it.

Her eyes were dark, her grip so tight that his fingers started going numb. "Remember. Once you do this, there is only one way to return your mortality. True love alone can break this covenant. And in that, there's—"

"I know, I know, there's a price, right?"

The woman released him, wagging a knobby finger as he left her hut. "Mostly correct, young man, but true love is—"

And he never heard the rest, not that he cared to.

A droning sigh filtered into the silent library like a fog settling around Xanthe's feet, making the spacious room even colder.

She was bored. Thousands of texts and tomes, and the only thing she could think about was how she'd run out of vermilion paint. Again.

She'd have read the library's contents, but frankly she was afraid they'd fall apart if she touched them. Painting was more relaxing anyway.

Her host once offered to read with her, but he seemed to have forgotten how. She wasn't surprised; it was probably difficult for him to grab books, turn pages, and remember to breathe properly to keep from ruining them. After the dust she'd encountered the first time in the library, he explained that his last tenants weren't interested, and it had been many years since he'd been in the room himself. Probably decades. Maybe a century. She could only guess. He was so ancient they had legends about him back home.

Staring at her half-finished work, she knew she shouldn't bother him. But it was an emergency.

"Canicus?" She whispered. Her voice carried on the invisible wings of mute spirits, echoing off the castle walls and assuring that she felt smaller and more alone than before. He would hear her though. He always did.

The castle rumbled and groaned like a woman in labor. It trembled periodically, more and more intense in the throes of its contractions. Xanthe knew when he reached the doorway. The trembling stopped, and the creature the castle birthed into the library was greater and more terrible than all his legends suggested.

His head entered: the tapered snout, square jaw rippling with savage muscle, and the orange reptilian eyes, each the size of a carriage wheel. His long, scaled neck wove in after it, and the claw of his wing clacked on the floor to keep his balance.

The great silver beast of the mountain.

When he spoke, the scent of ash and smoke billowed into the library, and his voice, even speaking softly, sounded like thunder. "Princess?"

His massive eye's gaze burrowed into her like a vortex of flames. Whenever she saw him, she couldn't help shrinking into herself and wringing her paint-stained hands together. "Um, I'm out of vermilion. I can't get a rose's luster without it."

Canicus' head swung away and he left wordlessly. The faint shuddering of the castle with his steps was the only reminder that any living thing resided on these desolate mountains.

Xanthe sighed again, her fingers caressing her canvas. Her heart full of longing, she allowed her solitude to swallow her.

Xanthe read the latest letter repeatedly until twilight, when she hid it beneath her pillow with the others. She had sent off her reply with the dove a few days prior. She still felt so lonely. She stared at the ceiling, unable to sleep for fear of the beasts that always laid in wait to prey on her dreams.

Wind rattled the windows of her tower chamber, signaling Canicus' return. She hopped up and scurried down the spiraling stairs, still in her dressing gown. Who cared? He was a giant silver reptile who'd been around since before the common folk had cutlery.

Xanthe was never sure how he fetched the things she asked of him. Some agreement with the locals, perhaps, since he always arrived with a bag slung across his mighty chest.

Canicus dipped his great head at her approach into the entry hall, then crouched to let her dig through his bag.

Xanthe withdrew the paints, along with some fresh bread he'd picked up for her. She clutched the items to her chest and scampered to fetch her canvas. Midway, she stopped and turned to her scaled warden. "I can't sleep. Will I see you in the solar room?"

Canicus nodded, and Xanthe continued on her new quest.

Xanthe leaned against Canicus' shoulder while she worked. The hearth was warm, but heat also radiated between Canicus' scales, and it felt nice on her back. She knew he watched her paint, but the company was welcome nonetheless.

Even when he chuckled about it. Deep rumbling, like the distant threat of a storm.

She pouted. "You promised you wouldn't laugh anymore …"

Canicus lifted his wing awkwardly. "Apologies. You're just such an awful painter."

"Then why do you keep bringing me paint?"

"Because you love it so much."

Xanthe blinked at him, clueless how to respond to his steadfast amber eyes. After a pause, she glanced away and Canicus spoke again. "I ran into your father on my way back."

Xanthe's paintbrush halted, and she glared holes into her canvas. "I don't want to see him."

"He misses you."

"I don't care." She didn't have much courage, but she allowed herself one outlet for her anger. It was his fault. Now she wasted away in a castle older than her kingdom with a monstrous warden probably just as ancient.

Canicus noticed her souring mood. "Apologies. I did not mean to upset you."

At least her jailer was a good companion. She resumed painting, her paintbrush seeking the shape of the face she loved most until the weight of her eyelids overcame her inspiration.

Canicus missed hands. More than anything, he missed having hands. A claw attached to each colossal wing wasn't the best appendage to pluck a tiny canvas out of a sleeping girl's grasp without rupturing it. The idea of using his teeth was worse. He was excellent at controlling his flames, but using teeth for such delicate actions was still beyond him, and paint tasted disgusting.

To say nothing of carrying her to a sleeping area. He could've done it if she was wearing something ... heavier. A dressing gown was *not* substantial enough to get a good grip without hurting her or ripping anything.

Xanthe had a habit of painting in her dressing gowns, claiming she didn't want paint on her good dresses, even when he brought aprons home to protect those very dresses.

He wasn't sure if he was thankful for his reptilian form or frustrated. She was comfortable because she didn't see him as a man, and she was right. He was a beast, a form which offered him sanctuary from any physical reactions his body may have had in human flesh. And no matter how many times he said it was improper, she would shyly apologize, saying it was only him.

Canicus never had the heart to argue, so he eventually dropped the issue entirely.

Her falling asleep like that, though, was a problem. Xanthe would be sore, he couldn't take her anywhere, and he couldn't bring himself to disturb her. So he flushed heat through his scales, curled his head and wing around her, and offered her comfort in dreams.

Another nightmare. They always started the same, a desolate wasteland filled with decay and monuments of the fallen from eons ago. Sometimes someone would come and the nightmare would cease, but others ended in all forms of torturous death Xanthe's brain could concoct.

Tonight, that someone came for her again. She never got his name, but he always felt familiar. He'd show up through a doorway of flames, as if the fire curled at the edges of her dream like kindled parchment. Usually all he did was sit with her, and eventually the wasteland turned into something else vaguely familiar—a place she knew, but not that place at the same time—as dreams often do.

"You're here."

"Another nightmare?"

She rolled her lips under her teeth. "Sorry."

"It's not your fault. It's probably more mine than anything."

"What?"

He shook his head. "Nothing."

He was handsome, yet undeniably chilling. His jaw was always set and his brows drawn, so ferocity dominated his face. But she was never afraid. Her nightmares were far more terrifying than long silver hair and orange eyes.

Xanthe slumped on the rocky ground and her guest sat nearby. It almost made her lonely, how he would never cross that invisible threshold. Like a ghost, he was always present, never close enough to stop her loneliness, but never far enough away to make her forget he was there.

A gilded cage even in her dreams.

"Want to talk about it?" He asked.

"You ever feel trapped?"

His fierce brow furrowed in time with his deepening frown. "Are you all right? Do you need help?"

Xanthe sighed. "Not like that. It's ... complicated. My living situation could be worse, but, inside, I feel ... like I'm still dancing to someone else's strings."

He paused, likely gathering up thoughts derived from her subconscious. After all, he was just a dream.

"To answer your question, I've felt trapped before, yes. Even now. But my prison is my home. My body. My life. So I do empathize to some extent." He glared at his hands, then shook his head. "I'm sorry. I wish there was more I could do for you."

Xanthe folded her hands together. "This is enough. Thank you, friend—can I call you friend? It's been so long and you've never told me your name ..."

A stray breeze intruded on their conversation, whipping his hair around his face and lifting his bangs so she could see his eyes. They were wide, blinking like the flickering of a candle in the breeze. His toughened, unreadable expression resurfaced, accompanied by the clearing of his throat.

"If you wish."

And that was that. Her nightmare faded, and the tide rolled in. The wasteland became a beach, and they listened to the waves until reality returned to claim its due.

For the first time in decades, Canicus opened the doors to the ballroom. There was only so much cleaning he could do, but the princess was intent on picking up the slack. Or so it seemed.

Xanthe wore a gown this time, so she clearly wasn't worried about soiling it. She twirled around the ballroom, humming, a broom serving as her dance partner.

How cute.

"What are you doing?"

The girl squealed, dropping her broom and gripping her heart to keep it from spiriting off without her.

Canicus rumbled. "My apologies. I thought you'd hear my approach."

Xanthe smoothed her golden hair as though calming a startled cat. "I was distracted. This room is beautiful."

"I thought you'd like it."

"Why'd you keep it hidden all this time?"

His wings ruffled. "I sometimes forget it exists. But I thought it might make your world a little bigger ..."

She studied him, and his skin shifted uncomfortably, as if she'd seen too much. The girl broke the silence, pointing to a massive hearth at the end of the ballroom. "Why don't we use this? It's much bigger than the one in the solar room!"

Canicus shook his head. "It is, but its purpose is different. I only light this when it's time to return wards to their people. My fire alone burns red in this hearth, and red smoke plumes into the sky—a call to retrieve the ward I guard."

She considered this and sought his eyes. "Then, will you someday light this for me?"

Canicus wasn't sure how to respond, and something in his chest clenched. "Yes. Until then, you are under my protection."

"I see."

Another indecipherable statement.

The threat of awkward silence loomed, and Canicus warded it off. "I shouldn't impose on you any longer."

As he turned to exit, she blurted out, "Wait!"

Canicus stopped.

"You can stay, if you want ..."

He smiled. "Very well, Princess."

It'd been days since he informed Xanthe about an appointment with her father, and she was still angry. It was obvious by how she walked. Her footsteps, usually feathers against the ground, plodded down the mountain like those of a prisoner to the gallows. Her father insisted on speaking alone, and Canicus refused to leave them undefended. So he flew to the edge of his territory to let the princess and the king converse outside it—a solution he wasn't happy with, but he could stand guard.

It made Canicus uneasy, being unable to hear or smell anything beyond his territory. What happened within those borders were the only things he could control. But they deserved to talk. And he could still keep her safe. It was his job, after all.

Canicus felt the peel of the tether splitting like wet leather. From the way Xanthe tensed when she left his territory, he guessed she could feel it too. He could sense danger afoot from anywhere, but once she left his boundaries, his heightened senses concerning his ward dissolved.

Canicus watched, unable to hear their conversation beyond his invisible fence. It looked like an argument. She was upset. He didn't need the tether to sense that.

When their confrontation ended, they both stepped into his realm, and the tether latched to his ward again. Xanthe thundered past him while her father approached, bearing a satchel.

"Thank you, again, Great Canicus of the Mountains, for guarding my daughter during these trying times."

"It's what you pay me for, Your Majesty."

The king frowned. "My health is failing, Canicus. My kingdom is threatened. They set their sights on the heir to the throne. They will come for her."

Canicus straightened to his full height and flared his wings. "Your Majesty, I've done this for many generations, and I've been master of these lands even longer. This mountain is painted in the blood of armies."

The king handed over the satchel and left. Canicus wasn't about to tell him that his duties weren't something he was proud of anymore. But they were the only things he still knew how to do. Protect. Defend. Scatter the ashes of some unsuspecting pompous fools across the mountainside.

But he was concerned. The second the king had entered the territory, a waft of darkness had tickled Canicus' nostrils. It was mild, clinging vaguely to the king's clothing like the perfume of a mistress. It fizzled out entirely when the king descended the mountain.

No sooner had they landed at the castle entrance than Xanthe stormed through the doors and up to her tower. He had seen family issues in his wards before, but with her, it was such a shame.

Canicus skulked into his dungeon lair and dumped the satchel onto his rolling hills of treasure. He lay on his bed of riches and rubbed his face against the coins. The jewels echoed beautiful melodic notes, and the smell soothed him, though not enough to keep his thoughts at bay. The charred skeleton in the corner made sure of that. He kept it as a reminder every time he was foolish enough to remember his humanity. He was a beast, for defense and devastation.

He had power to rule his land forever, just as he wished.

And it was dreadfully boring.

His only excitement was his status as a glorified bodyguard. Canicus hid their loved ones, important figures, and prisoners away until the clients deemed it safe to retrieve them. He had liked some wards well enough, but never was he close to whatever "true love" nonsense the old, scarred woman had said.

However, somewhere along the line, something had shifted. They weren't just wards anymore. Xanthe wasn't just his ward. It wasn't that she was more special than the others that came before.

No, something in *him* had changed. He wasn't the same anymore.

The scent and sound of treasure no longer made him feel rich, the scars he could inflict upon the landscape no longer made him feel powerful, and tales of his might no longer made him proud. It was all old and meaningless.

He paid everything for this prison.

"Canicus?"

Xanthe's whisper came through the thrum of their tether, and he reached out his cognizance to feel along its strands. He was always vaguely aware of her whereabouts, but he only intruded upon necessity.

She was in the solar room with her paints, and she'd want him to light the hearth, at least.

His instincts objected at abandoning his hoard when he slid his jaw off the jeweled bed. Despite the protests of his monster shell, Canicus deserted the hollowed dungeons of gold for the company of a princess.

Canicus didn't know why he laid behind Xanthe every night while she painted. He'd felt protective over wards before, and this feeling was different.

He didn't love her, did he?

He couldn't feel any desire towards her in this state. But she smelled like light: cool and clean, almost the way he thought the beach might smell. She was so small, so fragile. Gentle and soft spoken, always afraid of asking for anything, as though she were a burden. The only time she showed her steel regarded her family.

Canicus certainly felt endeared to her, but more than that, he wanted this skittish, lonely young woman to be happy.

Was that love?

If any of these things did border on love, would allowing himself to walk that path free him from his scaly prison? Was that something he wanted? He'd lost everything for this life, and he'd probably have to pay with this life to have it all back.

His territory, his hoard, his livelihood. He'd been a monster so long, the world hurtling by without him. He'd forgotten how to be human.

Even if he were ready for such a thing, he didn't know the requirements for breaking the covenant. He hadn't stayed to find out from the old woman. Did "true love" need to be reciprocated? Or could he become human again on his own?

Canicus leaned over to peek at her canvas. It was outlined in what was supposed to be roses, probably, and she worked on a human face in the middle.

Whoever Xanthe was painting, it wasn't him.

He wasn't sure why that revelation made his chest knot up. It was silly. It wasn't as though she knew what his human form looked like. Even if she recalled her dreams, she wouldn't know who he was.

Something about the whole situation unnerved him. "What are you painting?"

Xanthe glanced at the gargantuan burning eye beside her, then stared at her work, her finger tracing the person's face. "Someone I haven't seen in a long time ... I miss him so much."

Canicus felt a prick of guilt for being the lock on her birdcage. "Apologies. I wish there was something I could do."

Something must have cracked then, like winding a music box all the way only to keep turning. Xanthe set the painting aside and rested her head on her knees. He smelled the salt of her tears before he saw them, and settled his head beside her. She clung to his lip and leaned on his jaw.

"Rest, Princess. You are not alone. You are not alone."

"You are not alone."

His warmth must have followed her in dreams, for when she opened her eyes, an arm wrapped around her shoulders and a structured jaw leaned against her head, ruffling her golden hair.

Strands of a feathered silver mane danced across her sightline, and she knew her dream friend had returned. But when she turned to look, he was standing a few meters away in his sleek black coat.

"I'm sorry, miss." He pursed his lips, darting his face away as he dipped his head in an awkward bow. When he rose, his forehead creased and his eyes swam around in his sockets, drowning in some attempt at resolve.

"You're usually so distant. Why not today?"

His whisper was quiet but firm. "You seemed sad."

She rolled her lips under her teeth. He was only a dream, so speaking her mind couldn't hurt, right? "Then, will you hold me?"

He gave her that bewildered stare again.

"Please?"

Her dream-guest approached, and she closed the gap, wrapping her arms around his middle.

"Please don't leave me," she whispered into his coat. "You're all I have left. Without you I'm alone in my nightmares."

He tentatively embraced her and leaned his chin on her head. "I told you. You're not alone. Here or on the other side."

"I know, but I'm so afraid. I've lost my freedom, my love, my family ... one day you'll disappear, and the nightmares will come back."

The man stroked her hair gently. He didn't answer, but his warmth was comforting. Xanthe curled into the man's black coat and absorbed every bit of solace he was willing to give.

Canicus' eyes shot open like igniting flames. The palace was dark, and his tether stretched thin. She wasn't in the castle. He'd had countless runaway attempts before, but Xanthe had never tried.

Something was wrong.

He didn't sense intruders, but he felt a crawling tension, a tingle of claustrophobia, like a cell with no windows or doors—only the knowledge that one wasn't alone.

Canicus lumbered through the castle, bursting through the doors and taking to the sky the second he had room enough to spread his wings. He trailed his cognizance along the thin line of their tether, and felt worms of dread picking at his stomach.

He had to find her.

Xanthe shivered. The mountain was much slower on foot and her stolen pair of boots, likely from a previous ward with much bigger feet, slid on the snow. Guilt gnawed at her gooseflesh, the shame a devoted companion to the chill of the wind.

She would've said goodbye, but he'd try to stop her. This was her only chance. Spurred by her longing, she brushed off the nagging notion to return to the castle.

He'd be at the end of this empty mountain. He'd promised.

Xanthe found the edge of Canicus' territory, as she could feel his tether hanging by a few threads. She stared at the invisible gate to the wilderness beyond. The mountainside was peppered in young evergreens sprouting amidst the carbonized corpses of its predecessors. A prominent boulder overlooking a ridge made this place the perfect rendezvous point. The ridge even had a mountain path tracing its contour. She had made sure to mention it in her letters. To anyone else, it was a scenic route. To her, this was the edge of her enclosure. Once she walked through, she'd be free, but she wouldn't be safe anymore.

Terror shot up her spine.

Her hands shook, and her swallow felt heavy in her throat.

Why was she so afraid?

Xanthe dusted the snow from the boulder and sat in its grooves, arranging her stolen cloak to keep warm and camouflaged against prying orange eyes. The pull of the tether should alert her if Canicus was close, but she couldn't help scanning the skies and scouring the hem of the forest.

The sun breached the horizon and she was still waiting, queasiness shaking her stomach. She was almost out of time, and nothing had crested the mountain path.

Just as her faith failed, a voice hailed her from beyond.

"Ho! My love!"

Her heart leapt in time with her body. A silhouette rose with the dawn from the horizon, traipsing fearlessly along the ridge and straight towards her. Joy overcame whatever fear Xanthe had about crossing the barrier, and she leapt from the boulder and bolted down the mountain. She slid to a stop in the snow and gripped her hands tightly together to stop herself from jumping into the arms of her beloved right in the middle of the path.

The last warning of the splitting tether barely registered in her mind.

Her man stood before her, his wild dark hair and clean beard in stark contrast to his blinding smile. He wore a dashing cloak and a crossbow slung across his back. His armor gleamed in the remaining light.

"Sir Werther! I thought I'd never see you again! You got my letters!"

He ran his hand through his hair. "When your father's soldiers divulged your location, nothing could keep me away. Not him, not some fiery beast! You and I are destined, my love. When you summon me, I come."

A sigh bubbled over her jubilant heart. Xanthe stepped into his embrace, just in time to hear an ear-splitting screech from the sky.

The Great Beast of the Mountain descended upon them.

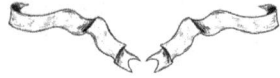

Canicus landed like an earthquake, eyeing the pretentious rat holding his ward. His voice rose with warning. "Return to the castle. It isn't safe."

Xanthe wouldn't look at him, but she clenched her dress in her fists and twisted the fabric. She bit her lip so hard Canicus was sure she would start bleeding. Her body was shaking, but her feet stayed rooted in the snow, unwilling to move. Her companion looked familiar, though Canicus had never seen him before. The man took her chin and sought her gaze. He said something, but the barrier blocked Canicus' hearing, so he could only guess the words.

Canicus itched to roast the man's entrails and knock them off the mountainside, but Xanthe's affection for the cocky brute stayed his flames. Yet the burning urge to drag her back inside the territory, to hold her and keep her safe, devoured him.

When they both entered his domain, unease crept up Canicus' spine, made worse by how Xanthe smiled in the man's arms. The man held up a peaceful hand, his other arm wrapped around Xanthe's shoulders. "I believe we have a grave misunderstanding. Let's sit and talk."

A distinct scent assaulted Canicus' nostrils, and his instincts flared. He roared, "Your Highness, get behind me! That boy reeks of darkness!"

Xanthe jolted, her gaze shooting to her companion's face. A vicious smile broke the man's pleasant façade. He whipped out a dagger and roughly jerked her into a tight hold in front of him. Then he pressed the blade to Xanthe's neck and used her as a shield. If it weren't for her, Canicus would've incinerated the boy where he stood.

She froze, barely breathing. "W-Werther? W-what are you doing?"

The fragility in her voice shot tingles of rage through Canicus' bones. Anyone who made her voice tremble like that deserved to be charcoal.

"Are you really that dim? You honestly thought I went through all the motions to court an unavailable princess only for the old codger to panic and hire a monster to keep the throne out of reach?"

"I don't understand. What's going on, my love?"

If she had not loved the pest, he would have been ash the moment his foul stench traipsed into range. Canicus felt the glands at the back of his throat leaking the flammable gas. All he'd have to do would be inhale and exhale deeply and Xanthe would be standing before a pile of soot. But he couldn't bring himself to do it while she trembled in her oversized boots.

"It's a miracle you haven't figured it out," he laughed.

Canicus snarled, "How will killing the princess grant you her kingdom?"

"So it's the beast that has the brains! Allow me to enlighten you, big white brute." The man's face turned predatory. "I'm not the one that's going to kill her. You are." He paused long enough to drink in Xanthe's horrified expression. The deplorable swine. "Or, that's how it's going to look, anyway. Your reputation will fall to ruin, beast, and the continent will demand your death. In the wake, a single hero will arise to slay the menace and be richly rewarded for avenging the death of the king's only child."

Canicus watched his shy, spirited ward's face flood with fury and betrayal. She stomped on her captor's toes, jamming her elbow into Werther's stomach the second the knife dropped from his hand.

Xanthe grabbed her skirts and ran towards Canicus. She slipped and fell face first into the snow. At the same moment, Werther grabbed his crossbow and aimed ... right at Xanthe's back.

She wouldn't be able to stand up in time.

Werther sneered, "You see, monster, I know your weakness."

The time to think had passed.

Canicus' wings tore across the space between them. He launched himself over Xanthe's head and landed above her, spraying snow over the ridge and casting a great shadow on his ward. Crouching, he dug his claws into the earth and spread the membranes of his wings like great ramparts. His head swung down, his posture aligning to fry Werther on his level. Canicus shielded the woman's body with his own and heard her whimper as the gas for his flames poured into his mouth.

Werther fired.

Something burning bore into Canicus' eye as half his vision violently ceased. It was over.

His last passing thought was the worry that his corpse would crush Xanthe.

Canicus was dead before he hit the ground.

His tether viciously shredded itself from Xanthe's spirit, and she screamed.

He crashed to one side, his wing still sheltering her. His body draped across the path, his head curled in an unnatural position and his monstrous tail draped down the ridge. Loose drifts of snow scattered around him. Xanthe fumbled to get to her feet and maneuver over the drifts to kneel beside his snout, her hands shaking with the fear of touching him.

So long as she didn't touch him, it wasn't real.

A click and the crunching of snow startled her. Sir Werther stepped closer, his crossbow locked with another bolt aimed at her heart. Instinctively, she turned and hugged Canicus' fallen jaw.

It was over.

There was nothing left.

Heat coursed through the scales under her fingertips. Xanthe's eyes shot open.

Could it be?

No, it wasn't the same as the gentle heat that kept her warm in front of the hearth every night. This heat was fierce and unrelenting.

She scooted backwards on the frozen ground as Canicus' scales glowed white hot. One by one, they peeled off and disintegrated into sky bound fireflies, their remnants shimmering in the abyss above until they twinkled out of sight.

His skin began to burn, fanning into an inferno that forced Xanthe to shield her face. She struggled to stretch towards him, desperately grasping to reclaim her routine monotony. She could accept all of it, if her only real friend was still alive.

Canicus' body burst in a shockwave of light and heat. It blew Sir Werther back with such force, it was impossible to tell if it sent him flying across the hills or vaporized him completely.

When the explosion subsided, Xanthe blinked rapidly and shook her head, her bleary sight warping with a myriad of woozy colors.

The dragon's carcass was gone.

What lay in its place seized her chest with rapid breaths. The beast's gargantuan, charred pelt, empty like a hunter's keepsake, sprawled across the land like a blackened scar on the mountainside. Amidst the angry sea of onyx and charcoal was a single snow drift.

What was that?

Xanthe tried crawling over to the drift, but the feeling of the scorched leather beneath her fingers shot uncontrollable chills up her arms.

Shriveling dead skin—

The horror rose in her belly and the substance of her nausea launched into her throat. Her hands flew to her mouth as she swallowed it down.

Xanthe stood and took small steps on shaking feet toward what she had assumed was snow.

It was a human body.

Her ribs ached with the banging of her heart, a defiant maiden behind a locked door. Against all reason, her feet still moved towards the figure that was buried beneath the shreds of Canicus' burnt hide. She couldn't recall a single thought until she saw the person's face.

It was *him*.

The man from her dreams.

Her friend.

Except…

He wasn't a dream.

His body was pale, and likely bare, save for Canicus' husk that draped over him and shielded half his form from her gaze. His eyes were closed, but it was definitely him. Strong jaw. Silver hair. Even the bangs that obscured his face. Her heart ached for this inexplicable, tangible fantasy.

Why wouldn't her feet move?

A breath shuddered through the man's lungs. The sound unlocked her legs, but sucked her strength out with it. The limbs collapsed under her. She crawled towards him, too undone to feel the coat beneath her fingertips anymore.

When Xanthe reached him, she shakily brushed the hair from his eyes. Upon seeing his face, she froze and instantly tore her gaze away from the bloody mess where one eye should be. The same injury that Canicus had just endured to save her.

She shook away the possible ramifications. Somehow, he still lived. She felt no link, no tether, but this man was alive. For now. Each weak breath inched him closer to the edge. She carefully gathered his head in her arms, gently peeling the rest of the hair from his face. The man drifted back to consciousness and he wheezed a groan, his remaining eyelid opening groggily to reveal an eye like fire. The truth was undeniable.

"C-Canicus?"

The eye darted to her, his brows knitted in that severe expression she had never seen in the waking world but was so familiar she could have painted it blind. Then his face shifted to add pain and confusion. "Princess? Why do you look so sad? I don't feel the— Am I …

dreaming? Why does it—?"

He winced, cutting himself off.

Xanthe stroked his bangs back as they fell over his face again. Her voice croaked. "You're not dreaming, Canicus. I can't feel the tether either. It's gone. You're ... human?"

Canicus' eye widened, and he lifted his hand and flexed his fingers, his visage painted in awe. "I'm human again ..."

Xanthe broke. Tears poured unhindered from her eyes. Her frantic, faulty inhales warred against her need to talk to him. "All this time? It was you, all this time?"

"Are you disappointed, Princess?"

She violently shook her head, no longer able to speak.

"That's a relief."

"Can—" she choked. "Canicus?"

He wiped the tears from her cheeks with his thumb, and blinked when the motion smeared blood across her face. He drew his hand away. "My apologies."

She grabbed his wrist and brought his palm back to her cheek as she cried. "Canicus, does it hurt?"

His eyelid drooped, and she saw a trace of something she didn't want to see. Resignation. He recovered and stroked her cheekbone. "Don't worry about that, all right?"

She cried harder.

He was slipping away.

He whispered to himself, seemingly amused. "So the condition for breaking it is the price, huh? How ironic and fitting."

Xanthe swallowed. "We have to go. Come, I'll help you."

His eye sought hers. "Princess."

She started wrapping her arm around him.

"Princess," he protested.

She violently shook her head and scrunched her eyes shut, for she was afraid of what he would say.

He gripped her arm with attempted firmness. "Xanthe!"

Her heart seized, and she finally looked at him. His severe expression returned, forced and weak though it was, his lone eye daring her to avert her gaze. "You're free now. It sounds unsettling, but you need to tear some of this skin. Wrap it around you. It should keep you warm. Go back to the castle. Light the hearth in the ballroom and throw the pelt into the fire. The smoke will turn red. There should be enough food in the pantries until the townspeople come for you."

Fury and sorrow burst from her throat in a strangled, guttural yelp. "No!"

She couldn't lose her only friend a second time in less than an hour. It was unbearable.

"Don't—" he began, his voice filled with compassion.

"Don't, Canicus! I'm going to cry and you cannot stop me!" She sobbed. She clutched his hand, and he wrapped his fingers through hers.

"Why? Why did you do it? This goes beyond your duty …"

Canicus shook his head. "If you had been my ward alone, I would have died a dragon."

He lifted their entwined hands and brushed the back of his against her face. "Yet, I've been gifted a few extra moments. It would be ungrateful to wish for more."

"Then call me ungrateful! Call me greedy, I don't care!"

"I would sooner call you kind, and gentle, too pure for this place. I would sooner watch you paint again and see you smile. But I am thankful, that I could see you, hear you, and feel your touch, as myself, just this once." His breathing grew weaker, as if he was trying to say everything he needed to before … "Be happy, my friend," he finished.

And all too suddenly, he was gone.

The breath of life left him, and he dissolved into bits of light. Frigid, lonesome air rushed into the spaces between her fingers. The weight of his head and softness of his hair in her other hand vanished, and her hand jumped in the unwelcome shock of emptiness.

Xanthe was so cold. She lifted the gargantuan, blackened hide and bundled it around herself to pretend her warmth hadn't just floated into the clouds. Then she doubled over and wept, huddling in it. Disgusting or not, the pelt was warm, like he said. And it still smelled like smoke and cinders, just like Canicus.

Soon she'd have to return to the castle and face the notion of throwing the pelt into the flames. That once-beautiful skin—the suit worn by a man trapped inside a monster—would shrivel and crumble into ash. And that would be all that was left of him.

But she couldn't bear the thought of the future at the moment. So she curled herself up in the past for as long as she could.

A thought made her soul ache. He said she was free.

She was free. But she was also, well and truly, alone.

The colossal doors screeched on their hinges. The queen paid them no mind. This creaky old castle couldn't scare her away. She thought raiders would've come, but clearly a deep magic still held over this place, warding off unwelcome darkness.

The queen's guard stood outside, as ordered. Despite their protests, she alone would enter this fortress. Dust stirred and peeled before her, paving a path for her presence. She marched through the halls with grace, her feet like feathers against worn woven carpets, even while she brandished her massive offering. A bottle of ash clinked around her neck.

Every turn she took with purpose, until she came to a mammoth entryway. A ballroom lay beyond, immense and untouched—at its end, a hearth so large a carriage could fit within it. The queen approached, each step echoing endlessly throughout the room like the whispers of spirits. Delicately climbing the hearth's stepped stone, she nestled her offering in a crook on its mantle.

When she'd finished, she picked her way down and admired her work. The painting she'd placed boasted a flying silver beast and a handsome man with long silver hair and orange eyes.

"What I wouldn't give for you to tell me how bad this painting is, my friend. My subjects only cast awe and admiration at my feet because of my station, not my talent. But it took me years to finish this one." She gave a wry chuckle. "It's probably awful, but it's the best I've got."

The queen stared forlornly up at the painting. Her hand clutched the bottle at her neck. "I miss you so much, Canicus. I'm so sorry. If I hadn't been such a fool, you'd still be alive."

"Wrong, my dear!" A high voice cackled.

The queen jumped to find an old woman with gnarled hands standing behind her. The stranger wore patchwork rags that matched the strips of fabric wrapping her fingers. She was diminutive and hunched, but in a deliberate way that made it unclear if her posture was by age or by choice. Her curly gray hair rebelled against the headscarves and braids that attempted to tame it. The woman would have been entirely overlooked in a poor village, but in derelict castle, she simultaneously looked entirely out of place and every bit at home.

"How did you—how did you get in here?" The queen stammered.

The old woman waved her off. "I have my ways, dear. Not important. What I am interested in, though, is that bottle around your neck."

When the old woman pointed to it, the queen held the bottle tightly, her expression hardening. "Who are you? And what did you mean, I'm wrong?"

"Again, not important, dearie. But I know who *you* are. And you're wrong if you think your behavior could've saved him."

"What do you mean?"

"It wasn't the crossbow that killed him," the woman explained flippantly, meandering around the ballroom, "He traded his humanity for immortality. That wound wouldn't have been fatal. Lost an eye perhaps, but …"

"I don't understand …"

The old woman stopped wandering and crossed the room to stand before the queen. She pointed a gnarled finger at the queen's chest. "The only way to break that covenant was true love. True love is sacrifice, my dear." The woman's gaze burned into the queen's eyes. "Protecting you at that moment, at the expense of his life, was no act of duty …"

Once more, Queen Xanthe was reduced to a tragic young girl, suffering the onslaught of grief and revelations she wasn't sure she wanted. She fell to her knees, even as the old woman adjusted her patchwork scarves and continued.

"Now that you know, I'm sure it's too much of a burden to haul those ashes around. Let me take all that pain off your hands."

Through her tears, Xanthe snarled, glaring as if looks were a means of execution. "This is all I have left of him. You won't take it."

The woman rubbed her temple. "Come, dear. I have a business to run. Just give me the ashes, and we can leave this behind you."

Xanthe stood and straightened, radiating a queen's dignity. "Take your offer and leave, permanently. I do not wish to forget, and I will not relinquish his ashes."

A cackle. "Why, would you look at that, my boy! You actually found a good one!"

"Who are you?"

The woman waved her hand dismissively and turned towards the exit. But when Xanthe swung her head, the woman was gone. Had any of their exchange even happened? But as she looked on the painting above the hearth, she knew.

She felt the weight of his sacrifice so keenly that she could hear his voice and feel his hands on her face. She still sensed the ghostly tingles of his tether by memory—or rather, the chilled pain of absence where his tether had once been, somewhere deep in her chest.

Canicus proclaimed her freedom, and yet, her heart had been dungeoned since his goodbye.

Years passed and the ache never left.

"I'm free and yet I suffer!" Her voice cracked as the tears caught in her throat. "I can't bring you back. The only thing I can do ... is live out my life until one day I can fulfill your final wish for my happiness."

The painting stared back in silence, and the castle echoed her mournful exclamation.

But somewhere deep inside her, painful warmth bloomed. Xanthe would carry his death wherever she went, but the cloak of his sacrifice had slipped, and she saw it now for what it was. She would hold onto that forever.

And for the first time in years, she didn't feel so alone anymore.

Young Death

Bethany A. Jennings

I'm leaning over my needlework when Young Death arrives again.

I feel him behind me at first, a rush of cold like a whisper across my spine and neck. My handmaidens, unaware of his presence, mutter about drafts in the palace and get up from their cushions on the floor to fetch their shawls. But I remain still in my chair, willing my heart to calm, letting my pulse quiet down from its inevitable race, steeling myself for whatever inquiry Death might have today.

After all, he is only a very Young Death. He's not the Elder Death, or the Middle Death. They all have their times, and Young Death will become them someday.

But for now, he is just himself.

Very young. Very inexperienced.

Very foolish to strike bargains with princesses.

"Good afternoon, Death," I murmur, sticking the needle through my embroidery. "What brings you here this time?"

"Illness in the palace, highness," his soft voice comes whispering back. He sinks to a seat beside me on a cushion—a specter clad in black from head to foot, large open eyes peering out at me from under a dark hood. If he was living, I'd gauge him to be my age. But his eyes have an innocence of darkness in them. A blindness that comes of not really knowing life, but being entirely sincere about it.

I press my lips in a firm line and nod, taking a moment to compose my response. It's always best to be cautious with Death. "Can you tell me whom?"

"The cook's son, highness." Death purses his lips.

"How old?"

"Not quite two years, my lady."

I hide the shudder in my heart and merely nod again. The more emotional I am, the higher I may need to drive the bargain. Eventually he may realize what a struggle this is. But for now, I still have him in the dark.

"Do you want to bargain?" He pulls his knees up under his chin, staring out at me, looking like a lost child.

Do I want to bargain? I swallow, silently adding more stitches to the golden flower in my cloth. This flower gains petals, while I lose mine ... one by one ... with each bargain I strike. That single touch from Death, each time, takes away a part of my soul and strength.

By the time I come of age, I will be nothing but a hollowed-out shred of a person, and then Middle Death will come and take me away.

Middle Death is not like Young Death. Middle Death is jaded. He has no reluctance. He is cruel and unyielding. And Elder Death is colder still.

But Young Death ... he does not want to do the work he does. And that is why he is willing to strike the bargains. In exchange for my silence on his cowardice, he will take my life for a life.

The cook's boy. Alas, I do not know the sick child, but I have met the cook. I have seen his haggard face in recent weeks. I know his wife was freed years ago from slavery to a comfortable home in this palace. But to lose her child after her former suffering ... such heartbreak.

When I die, who will mourn for me?

My brother, perhaps. But he will rise to the throne. And my sister after him. She and my parents do not even deign to visit me in my chambers. My handmaidens serve me only out of duty, never affection. No lover wants my sickly face. No prince or nobleman wants a princess who is confined to bed, who descends into weakness again and again.

I hate this life so much.

But I cast Death a quiet smile and place my needlework across my lap. In a few weeks I'll have the strength to take it up again. What are a few weeks of misery in exchange for a child's life?

I draw my last steady breath for a fortnight. "I'll take the trade. As usual."

His eyes pool with sorrow. "You're sure, my lady?"

Startled, I blink at him. Does he know how hard this is for me? I did not expect his compassion.

Nor do I deserve it.

When Middle Death comes for me, when I am finally one trade too far, I will divulge my secret. The trades Young Death has been dealing, the betrayal of his duty. Death will then turn against Death, and they will destroy each other, for they are uneasy allies, but impossible foes. And then we will have no Death left. None save the Elder Death, whose coming is, at times, a mercy.

Young Death does not know that my secrets will go with me to my grave—and there be revealed.

But his sincere, pale-blue eyes stare right into my soul, and my resolve falters. "I'm ready," I whisper anyway. *Don't drag this out. Don't make me doubt.*

"You say that you are ready," he murmurs, angling closer, "but I never am."

And instead of the cold touch of Death on my forehead or my cheek or my outstretched hand, this time he wraps his mouth around mine.

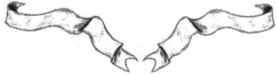

Recovery is slow.

I hear the maids spreading rumors about a miraculous healing in the servants' quarters. A little boy, not quite two, brought back from the brink of death. I only smile, nod, and drink the healing soup the cook sent up from the kitchen.

But that one afternoon of sitting and drinking soup is too much. The next I am taken with fever. The physician comes with his leeches and horrible medicines that I barely choke down. Even my parents come to visit for once, foreheads furrowing from the distance of my bedroom doorway.

Days and nights blur into an extended nightmare of sleep and dread and fire in my bones and mind.

When my birthday comes, I only know it from my brother, who comes to stroke a hand across my sweaty brow, and murmurs, "You're eighteen today. Stay with us. Please don't go."

I manage a heartsick smile.

Lying in this bed, day after day, I've realized that, for a very long time, I've been hoping my plan would fail—that I would die young, and it would be Young Death who comes for me, not his elders. That he would take the last of my life along with the rest I have traded and bargained away to him. That the last thing I know might be his kiss again, his open eyes, his very reluctant and gentle hands.

But I am the only one who can see the three Deaths, who can use my leverage over Young Death to tear them apart. To save my father's kingdom from their power. Or at least from all but the Elder Death, who I cannot touch.

To want to die young ... how very selfish of me.

I clench my hand around my pillow and hide my face in the silks so no one will hear me weep.

That night is a lucid night for me. Someone has opened my windows, and moonlight streams over my bed.

A shadow crawls across the upper windowpanes.

I catch my breath.

It's time. Time to betray Young Death. Time to give the last of my life.

Middle Death slips through the wall as easily as air, and treads to my bedside. He is heavy, broad, and shadows pour from his garments like smoke, darkening the shafts of moonlight over my coverlet.

Young Death has betrayed your cause.

I can't move my mouth.

Before you take me ... Young Death ... I have to tell you ...

My jaw feels frozen shut.

I've made a bargain with Young Death ...

These are words I cannot say.

My hands shake in my lap as Middle Death leans over the bed, a hungry smile reaching across his face.

I'm going to fail.

After all these bargains, all of this, I'm going to fail. I can't carry through my own plan. I can't betray Young Death. I can't watch him and this hulking shadow of darkness tear each other apart.

"You can see me," Middle Death observes, and runs his tongue across his teeth. "Do you know why that is?"

"Because I am about to die?" I croak.

But either that's a lie, or I've been on the brink of death my entire life.

Oh, why did it take me eighteen years to die?

"That's right," Middle Death replies, voice dry. "I am about to take you away. The life you have known is now worthless—a scrap of garbage. You have done nothing of value. You can take nothing with you. This is the end."

A voice rings out from the rafters above us. "You're wrong."

And Young Death drops down from the rafters, landing at the foot of my bed. He throws back his hood, his light eyes and snow-white hair reflecting the moonlight. "She has done everything, my brother. Others may see a broken princess bound to a chair, but she is the savior of dozens of lives."

Middle Death only sneers. "You think I don't know what you've been up to? Do you think I have been threatened by you not doing your work *properly*? What do you think happens to the young, if you do not take them at the proper time?"

My heart falters at the horror in Young Death's face.

"*I* take them. Or Elder Death does." Middle Death grabs me by the hair, lifting me from the cushions. His hand is like a ball of ice, sending needles of glacier-cold into my head and down my spine.

He shakes me, turning my face to look straight into his leering eyes. "And you. Did you think your act was a mercy? No, princess.

You have only granted these children longer suffering. Have you ever asked yourself why Young Death is so gentle? Is it because he deals with the most delicate and innocent? Faugh!" He spits, and his spittle stings cold on my shoulder. "It is because his crossings are a mercy. All death is a mercy, but especially at a young age, when they can be spared the suffering in the world."

I choke. "They have more *life*! To live and to do good things!"

"And then what? To fade out with my hand around their necks." Middle Death leans closer to me, and my vision begins to go dark as his hand closes around my throat. "Look at you here. Look at all this suffering you have endured. For nothing." He turns his gaze on Young Death, leering. "You should have taken her when you had the chance. Now she is mine. And I will have no mercy."

"You're wrong again." Young Death stands to his full height—much taller than I had expected, not slinking or creeping, but standing bold and tall, an inch or two higher than Middle Death himself. "Do you know what day it is, brother?" He asks, pale eyes suddenly glinting.

"Her eighteenth birthday," Middle Death growls. "She is of age, and she is mine."

A smile draws across Young Death's face. "It is my eighteenth birthday too, brother. I am of age. I can become the Middle Death—if I defeat you."

Middle Death throws me back against the pillows in rage.

"*That* is why she sees us, brother," Young Death cries, his hands spread out like an invitation to battle. "Her highness was born on the birthday of Death. The exact time that I died and became ... this. If we take her now, she will not pass on—she will become the Young Death herself."

Me. *Me*, a Young Death. Cold fear squeezes my heart. I will forever walk in darkness, forever taking lives, forgetting what I once was, becoming the specter of my subjects' worst fear.

"Then I shall take her," shouts Middle Death. "She shall replace *you*."

"No!" Fear and love mingle in Young Death's expression as he casts his gaze on me. "I have seen her soul, with every touch. I know her heart. I know her hope. I won't let her become what I am."

Middle Death growls in fury, and hurls himself in the air toward me—

And Young Death leaps into the gap. Taking the blow. Tossing Middle Death aside.

Death grapples with Death on the floor. The younger Death's blades dart in his hands, sharp and shining as icicles, and embed in the older's chest. Middle Death's crushing grip closes on the younger's throat. And then he pulls the icy blade from where it was embedded in his chest, and buries it back in Young Death's own heart.

Young Death staggers away. Light begins leaking from him—as if all that he is was a facade for the light of life, wrapped inside the trappings of darkness. On the floor, Middle Death bleeds out light, too, in puddles on the flagstones that rise instantly into a mist. He doesn't move. All the lives that he has taken are leaking out, coming back into the world.

My heart hammers, and I realize I'm crouching on the edge of the bed, about to fall off of it.

Young Death stumbles to my side, gently pushing me away from the edge. "You'll fall and injure yourself, highness," he whispers.

"You're ... dying." I swallow.

He falls flat on his back across the bed, beside me. I reach out, hesitating, and run a hand through his flyaway white hair, then trace over his prominent cheekbone, down to his angular chin. He's bleeding lives too—all the lives that were taken from our land before I was old enough to strike a bargain.

"Highness," he whispers, eyes full of light and pain and joy and agony, "this time *you* take the kiss."

"Won't I become the Young Death?" I cry.

He smirks a little. "Trust me."

My pulse hammers until I feel like I'm nothing but a heartbeat, a violent throb of delight and terror.

I wrap my arms around Young Death, and press my lips over his, trembling as I open up my whole soul.

Life surges into me.

All that Death has taken, every ounce over years and years, every life traded, every part of my strength, is mine again, pouring out from him and back to me. I gasp and draw away.

I'm a golden flower coming back to life, petals unfurling again where there was nothing.

My fingers glow. I feel my face—thin cheeks filled out to healthy fullness again—and my middle—once wasted away to harsh bone, now healthy and curved under my nightdress.

Young Death is now the faded one, his eyes sunken, his cheeks hollow.

"There is no Young Death in this kingdom. Not anymore." He has nothing left in him to smile with his mouth, but his eyes twinkle. "You gave yourself away to me piece by piece. But all your life is given back to you now, as you deserve, and I shall die instead."

"No," I cry. "Middle Death took you, once! Once Death took you too!"

Even as I speak, a strand of golden-white glow flies across the room from Middle Death, wrapping Young Death in light, sinking into his skin, surging through his veins.

I press another kiss to his lips, and this time they're warm. All of him is warm and soft in my arms—and strong and gentle as he wraps his embrace around me.

On the floor, Middle Death vanishes into dust. Gone, as though he never existed.

"What does it make you," I whisper, hugging him tight, "if you're born again on the death-day of Death?"

He pulls another dagger from his robe—the black fabric now a shifting, iridescent mesh of color that seems to have more hues the longer I gaze into its depths. Excitement spreads across his face. "You have seen Death. I have *been* Death. Young Death and Middle Death are no more, but one last Death remains."

With a strength I haven't had since childhood, I leap from the bed. "This kingdom does not need another princess on another throne."

He grins in full delight. "You will hunt the Elder Death with me!"

I wrap my hand around his, around the hilt of the dagger between his fingers. "We will slay him, you and I."

Both of us are tingling with life and energy, hardly willing to let go of each other's hands. I release him only for a moment, to jot a farewell note and seal it with my signet ring—signed to my brother, the only one who ever showed me care.

Then Death and I slip through the palace gates at dawn, unnoticed. The first gleam of sunlight glints golden off his blade. I revel in the chill of fresh air on my face and hands, the new strength in my limbs.

Later, the kingdom may mourn for me. Wonder what became of me.

But I am the princess who conquers Death, who takes Death by the hand. I trade myself for my people.

And nothing will stop our hunt until the final Death is dead.

Phoenix

Katherine Massengill

"It's too hot for a human blanket." Poking a spoon into the pan of stir fry, Michelle leaned into her husband's embrace anyway.

Terrence rested his hands on her hips. "Babe, it's forty degrees outside. And you're in a tank top."

She shrugged, giving him a quick kiss on the cheek before pulling away. "You know I'm never cold." Michelle glanced at the steampunk-style clock that hung on the wall over the cedar china cabinet. Their daughter Hannah had picked it out at age twelve. It didn't match anything in their kitchen, but Michelle treasured the way the quirky timepiece made Hannah smile.

"Why do you think I married you? I get my own personal space heater," Terrence said with a smirk.

"Very funny. Did you hear from Hannah?" As she spoke, Michelle pulled the wok off of the hot stove and turned the flame off. She washed her hands before pulling a large bowl of salad out of the fridge.

"She found a flight. She'll be home next Monday, after finals."

Michelle shook her head. "It feels like she should still be ten years old, painting the neighbor's dogs purple and giving herself a cootie-shot if a boy got too close."

Terrence laughed. "Or punching bullies in the face."

"Didn't we talk about not encouraging violence?" Michelle chided.

"You're the one who weaponizes spatulas any time I try to steal a cookie. I'm pretty sure she got her violent tendencies from you. Besides, that Price kid deserved it. Any boy who bullies people deserves to get hit by a girl."

He had a point. Hannah had definitely inherited her mother's temper, as well as her unique abilities.

He set the table, grabbed a bottle of sparkling cider, and pulled Michelle's chair out for her. As she sat down, he poured cider into both glasses.

Terrence sat down and said a quick blessing for the meal, then launched into an anecdote about his coworker throwing a football to him across the parking lot, and accidentally hitting the new supervisor in the face.

"I thought we were both dead," Terrence admitted with a sheepish grin. "He didn't get mad, though."

People never got mad at Terrence. Michelle was unable to keep a smile off her face even as she rolled her eyes. If they did get mad, it wasn't for long. He instinctively knew how to set people at ease, and had an almost psychic ability to know who he could tease, who needed gentler handling, and who to avoid. He also shared Hannah's antipathy toward bullies, a trait that Michelle admired even when it worried her. When they'd witnessed several thugs threatening a young boy, Terrence hadn't hesitated to intervene. He'd nearly been stabbed with a switchblade. But the would-be murderers fled, after Michelle threw up a wall of flame to protect her husband and the victim.

The hatred in the thugs' eyes and the heart-racing panic still triggered nightmares.

"Hey. Where'd you go?" Terrence's gentle voice caught her attention.

Michelle forced the terrifying memory aside. This was their anniversary. She should be thinking about happy things.

"Australia," she quickly responded. At age ten, she'd watched a documentary on the faraway continent, and had been fascinated ever since.

Terrence cocked his head to one side, and she knew he'd caught the lie. But he didn't push her.

"Ooh, scary spiders and giant sharks," he teased. "Sounds like the perfect vacation."

"The Sydney Opera House. Beautiful scenery," Michelle countered. She leaned forward, anticipating a playful argument.

"Their pizza tastes funny." Terrence twisted his face into a grimace. She rolled her eyes as she took a bite of stir fry. "How would you know? You've never been there."

"Court has. She took a work trip to Australia in May, and told me afterwards that the pizza was disgusting."

"Your sister is one of the pickiest eaters on the planet." There were five-year-olds who ate a wider variety of foods.

"She likes your stir fry," he pointed out, gesturing towards his plate.

"Only because I don't tell her what's in it. And as much as I love Courtney, I don't want to talk about your sister on our anniversary."

"Fair enough. But I guarantee you'll want to talk to her tomorrow." Michelle raised her eyebrows. "Okay, I'll bite. Why?"

"Because she can help you with the planning."

Mischief danced in his eyes as he pulled out a long, thin, gold-wrapped box from underneath his coat. Michelle unwrapped it and opened the lid to find two plane tickets lying inside. Tickets to Sydney, Australia.

"Terrence! We can't afford this," she blurted out. Her hands shook. "Hannah's in college, and we haven't paid off the house …"

"Hannah has a scholarship and is working a part time job," Terrence said. "And we'll still be able to make the house payments. I promise you, we can afford it."

"But how?" She asked, calming. "And how did you keep it from me?"

"I've been planning this for a year." He blushed. "Court helped."

"I take back half the bad things I ever said about her," she murmured.

"Happy anniversary, babe."

Unable to breathe from excitement, Michelle jumped up and ran around the table, hugging Terrence hard. He kissed her hair, returning the hug. She tilted her head back to look at him, and the joy on his face gave way to surprise and fear.

"Babe? Your eyes are glowing."

Michelle froze. *No, not now. This can't be happening now.* She ran to the mirror in the hall bathroom, heart in her throat.

Her dark brown eyes had turned amber. The Change was starting.

She clutched the sink to hold herself up as she started to hyperventilate. Flames smoldered under her skin, summoned by fear. Her heart pounded as they struggled to break free, immolating the flesh that imprisoned them. She smothered them into submission.

They couldn't have her, not yet.

Terrence walked over and stood behind her, resting his hands on her shoulders. She leaned into his embrace, shoulders shaking. Hot tears poured down her face. At least she was still human enough to cry. That wouldn't last long.

"We knew this was coming." Terrence's voice was barely a whisper.

"But it's too soon. Mother was fifty-three when she …" Michelle couldn't finish. She wanted to see her daughter graduate from college, maybe even fall in love. She wanted more time with Terrence.

Her husband stroked her hair, murmuring reassurances.

"Let's go sit down," he urged. He led her to their bed and curled up with her, their foreheads nearly touching.

"We still have a little time," he said, holding her close.

"Not much. A month, maybe two." Not nearly enough time. Twenty more years wouldn't be enough.

"I'll take however long we have."

He had to be hurting, but only his grey eyes hinted at the storm inside. The steadfast love on his face calmed her. Terrence had always been the rock that anchored her when anger or pain threatened to carry her away.

"We'll have to cancel the trip, and how do I tell Hannah …?"

Terrence put his finger to her lips. "We're not canceling the trip," he said. "We leave in two days, and we'll be back in a week. You've always dreamed of this. I'm going to make it happen."

Michelle sat up, twisting the sheet in her hands. "But we can't go now."

Terrence tugged the fabric away from her, sitting up as well. "Why not? I've already taken a leave of absence. We can pretend that you started feeling bad on the trip, went to the doctor when you got home, and discovered … some kind of illness. I'll take some more days off."

She hesitated. Her usually easy-going husband wasn't about to lose this argument. People called Michelle stubborn, but Terrence could give mules a few lessons in balking. He just chose his battles well. "Will your boss let you?"

He shrugged. "Probably. I still have time saved up, and I've put in a lot of overtime. Besides, you matter more than the job."

His boss would probably bend over backward to keep him onboard. Terrence loved his job, and was a stellar worker.

"But Hannah—"

"Still has exams to take," he interrupted, taking her hands in his. "We can tell her when she comes home. It'll be better for her to hear it in person."

"Okay," she whispered. "Let's go."

On their first night in Australia, they attended a concert at the Sydney Opera House. For several hours, Michelle forgot her fears, swept away by a mesmerizing concert. A couple days later, they traveled to Queensland. Terrence agreed to try calamari, but refused to take more than a few bites. They told stories about the past and present, avoiding the future by unspoken agreement.

Once or twice, Michelle saw Terrence wipe his eyes, but he smiled more often than not. Maybe some of it was a show, but most of it was genuine. Terrence loved life and had always kept focused on the present, enjoying each moment as if the next might evaporate in a breath.

They explored the Daintree Forest, and went snorkeling along the Great Barrier reef. She'd enjoyed both excursions, even though she'd nearly broken her nose when a wave knocked her off her surfboard. Terrence made sure she was okay, then laughed at her.

Today, they were swimming at a beach near their hotel. Earlier that morning, they built a large, elaborate sandcastle. Small shells adorned the walls, a shallow trench filled with water protected the castle from crab invaders, and a small scrap of cloth tied to a thick reed served as a flag. They raced each other, parallel to shore, using two large umbrellas as markers. Terrence won almost every time, but Michelle beat him twice.

"I need a break," she demanded with a laugh after her second win. She flipped onto her back in the water, squinting at the seagulls flying overhead. A brilliant sun shone in a nearly cloudless sky, its rays warming her blood and bones. The water seemed to lull her fire magic into a quiescent state; a welcome relief. Ever since her eyes had changed color nearly a week ago, her flames churned constantly inside her, seeking release.

Something bumped against Michelle's outstretched leg. She jerked away, startled, and stiffened as a large shark cruised by her. Michelle gently tread water, trying not to panic. She gasped in relief when it swam away towards the deep ocean.

"Let's go in," Terrence said. She turned in the water and saw his pale, terrified face.

"So, what do we have planned for tonight," Michelle asked once they reached the shore.

"Dinner, and then a sunset cruise," Terrence said as he took her hand. "I was thinking we could eat McDonald's."

"After paying for this trip, we'll be eating McDonald's for a month."

"Hannah offered to bring us some of her ramen noodle stash."

Michelle fought to keep a straight face. "Angling for good daughter points, I see. We'd better check her grades."

"Or find out if any annoying classmates have gone missing. She mentioned that she needed a shovel."

"Nonsense," Michelle said, waving her free hand in dismissal. "All she needs is a nice pile of dry wood."

A nearby couple gave them strange looks and moved away.

"It's a good thing we're going home tomorrow," Michelle said, "or half of Australia might become convinced we're serial killers."

"We can be the Sandcastle Killers," Terrence suggested.

"You're crazy," she scoffed, giving him a light shove.

He sidestepped, caught her outstretched arm, and spun her in a circle before pulling her to him. "And yet you married me."

"Do you ever wish you hadn't?" Her voice caught on the last word.

"Never," Terrence said, with a quiet fierceness.

"Even now?" She hated herself for the question. Her mother had skipped the wedding, but showed up at the reception to tell them they were making the biggest mistake of their lives. Michelle had dismissed her words as bitterness, but now she wondered if her mother had been right after all.

Terrence ran his hands down her arms and laced his fingers through hers, dropping to one knee. "You are my life, the light of my world, and the best part of me. I will never regret loving you, not if I live for a hundred years."

"Same here," she whispered. She didn't deserve this man, but she was glad he was hers.

As he stood, the intensity in his face lessened. A slow smile bloomed across his face, crinkling the laugh lines at his eyes. "Glad that's settled. Now, I believe there are some sandwiches in the cooler that are begging to be eaten. What kind would you like?"

Michelle relaxed in a chair on their hotel room balcony, letting the warm nighttime breeze dry her hair. Her camera sat on the table next to her bottle of water. She probably should take pictures, but what was the point? No need for mementos when you only had a month to live, and Terrence had never been one for photo albums. Right now, she simply wanted to exist.

She gazed up at the Southern Cross and other constellations she'd memorized from magazine pictures. The burning stars called to her, even as they frightened her. According to legend, phoenixes lived within them, beings of pure fire. Michelle's mother had told stories of a demigod who lured a phoenix down to Earth and trapped her in human form for fifty years. When she grew strong enough, she cast off her human form and returned to her family in the sky.

Like her legendary ancestress, Michelle's mother had always regarded her human form as a prison. She constantly insisted that their lives really began after the transformation. She had loved her daughter, but feared and distrusted nearly everyone else, bitter from the rejection of Michelle's father after he learned his wife's true nature.

But when Michelle tried to push Terrence away after her mother's transformation, he steadfastly refused to leave. He taught her to treasure each day, not let fears of the unknown hold her captive.

"Beautiful night," Terrence commented, stepping onto the balcony. He wore a t-shirt and shorts, and his hair was slightly rumpled from lying down in bed. Michelle smiled at him, and leaned over to kiss him on the lips when he sat down next to her.

"You got tired of vampires and Bigfoot?"

Terrence loved watching documentaries about the supernatural beings that shared their world. Michelle didn't share his fascination, and was glad that their town was mostly human. She'd never been sure how a vampire or fae might react to her.

"Tired of them? Never. But you're way more interesting."

He put an arm around her shoulders, lightly rubbing her back. She leaned into his hand, feeling the tension in her muscles relax just a little.

"Is something wrong?"

"Not wrong," Michelle said after a moment of thought. "I just needed to see the stars." She looked again up at the five stars of the Southern Cross, still beckoning her in the velvet sky. She turned her head away.

"If your mother's stories are true, you might see them up close and personal soon enough," he said, barely loud enough for her to hear.

Michelle studied his profile. Tension hardened his jaw and neck muscles. This was the first time he'd mentioned her impending transformation since her eyes had changed.

"But we have no way of knowing if those are true. I saw Mother fly up into the sky, yes. But afterwards? I don't know."

"You're afraid that the stories are wrong," he said, his statement almost a question at the end.

"Yes. What if there's no wonderful, loving community? Maybe

I'll spend eternity alone. Or maybe they'll all despise me."

"They'll love you. I'm sure they're counting the days, wondering when I'll stop being so selfish and send you to them." The edge of bitterness in his self-deprecating humor made her heart ache.

They both looked up at the sky, quiet for a minute. "I wish I could stay," Michelle whispered.

"I wish I could go with you."

They arrived at the Canberra airport at six a.m. Australian time. As they waited to board, Michelle kept fiddling with the necklace she wore; a phoenix pendant that Hannah had given her one Christmas. She longed to hold her daughter close, to see her bright smile. But the conversation they needed to have loomed over her, dark and threatening.

Hannah knew about the transformation, of course. Michelle had told her stories about phoenixes, all the legends her own mother had told her as a small child. She had taught Hannah how to control the innate abilities that phoenixes developed at the onset of puberty.

But understanding that the transformation would take place, and actually seeing it, were two different things. How do you prepare your child for being left behind? The transformation was a kind of death. Michelle would never see Terrence again. She couldn't even be sure that she would see Hannah again. All she had to go on were legends.

Terrence squeezed her hand. After twenty-five years of marriage, he knew when she needed comfort. Michelle stepped closer, reassured by his presence even when he didn't speak. The closer she got to home, the stronger her longing for her daughter grew.

Hannah waited for them at the Richmond International Airport, dressed in a black, rose-patterned skirt that skimmed her ankles, and a Renaissance-style blouse. Her curly brown hair tumbled down her back and around her shoulders, barely restrained by a headband with a phoenix on it.

The minute she spotted them, she ran over and threw her arms around Michelle.

"You're home, you're home! How was Australia? Did you have a good time? Did you see any kangaroos or sharks? Or did you guys spend all your time in the hotel?" She paused for breath. "Actually, don't answer that last one."

"I hadn't planned on it," Michelle said dryly.

The ever-irrepressible Hannah smirked. She was way too much like her father in some ways.

"Australia was wonderful," Michelle continued.

"Your mom scared off a shark," Terrence cut in, hugging his daughter and kissing her cheek. At five-eleven, Hannah was nearly as tall as he was. They made Michelle feel short.

"I did not scare him off," Michelle retorted. "We weren't bleeding, and we aren't seals."

Hannah turned back to her mother, her mischievous grin widening. Michelle braced herself for teasing.

But Hannah's face paled. "Oh, Mom," she murmured. "Your eyes."

Michelle swallowed hard, suddenly unable to speak. Deep inside her, the flames roared to a blaze.

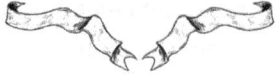

For the first week after they got home, the three of them spent as much time as they could outside. They went hiking on a weekend camping trip and visited the nearby park almost daily. Hannah talked about college, gushing about her favorite classes and her friends. She had a new roommate, Isabel, who apparently was a vampire.

"We bought two fresh cantaloupes, and she just bit into one with her fangs and sucked the juice out. I tried to get her to drink a coconut, but she said she doesn't like them." Hannah shrugged. "The blood bags in the fridge and freezer are kind of creepy, though. She wraps them in opaque paper, but once you know what they are, it's kind of hard to forget."

Hannah showed her a book of legends about phoenixes. Michelle reached out to take it, hesitating a little. She leafed through the pages, many of which had artistic designs hand-painted on the borders. Brilliant illustrations depicted phoenixes in human and fiery form.

"It's beautiful. Where did you find it?"

"The school library had it," Hannah explained. "Isabel said it matches some stories that the vampires have about us. And Mom, their records go back millennia. It sounds like some of those old legends might be true after all. Can you imagine?" She bounced a little on her chair, eyes shining.

"How are you so unafraid, when I'm terrified?" Michelle wondered out loud.

Hannah shrugged. "Horrors may fill the world, but wonders do too. You and Dad always taught me to seek out the wonder."

Her words rang in Michelle's mind for days. Seek out the wonder. The transformation was a change, yes. But change could be good. Marriage had been one of the best changes in her life, matched only by motherhood.

She couldn't let fear smother faith.

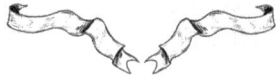

By week two, Michelle started to weaken. She got dizzy if she stood too quickly and exhaustion hit after an hour of exertion. Her moods fluctuated wildly. Sometimes she railed at Terrence and Hannah until they left the room or sometimes the house, although neither went very far. One was always within earshot. Other times she curled up in a ball, shuddering in misery. Even when she was calm, she felt horrible. Burning pain filled her body nearly every minute of the day. She couldn't eat, and sleep was a distant memory. Every day it got worse.

"I hate this," she burst out one day when she stumbled on the stairs, nearly falling. Terrence grabbed her around the waist, steadying her. Michelle swallowed hard against nausea.

Her husband kissed her forehead and linked his arm through hers, helping her down the stairs.

"Can't I just burn up without nearly dying first? Migraines are bad enough." Migraines were one of the few ailments that affected a phoenix. At least until the full transformation began.

"Well, you've been spared chicken pox, colds, and most of the illnesses that plague us poor humans," Terrence quipped.

"Not helping," Michelle grumbled. She felt too horrible to decide if he had a point. "Can you turn on the fan? It's steaming in here." The fan wouldn't help much, but his sweater made her itch, and it was too hot to be held.

The minute he let go of her, she wanted his arms around her again. Had her mother been this irrational? Michelle couldn't remember.

Terrence obediently turned on the fan. He went into the kitchen and came back after a few minutes, carrying two bowls of ice cream and two mugs on a TV tray. One mug held hot chocolate. Another held milk.

"When did you get ice cream?"

"Court brought it over. You were napping upstairs."

The ice cream was her favorite; chocolate chip cookie dough. Terrence sat down on the couch and tossed a blanket over his legs. Michelle put her feet in his lap. The blanket was nice and soft, and didn't make her skin itch. She wore a halter top and shorts, as little clothing as she could. Hannah wandered downstairs, carrying her tablet. She slouched in the recliner and played on her device as they watched a movie.

"Want some ice cream?" Michelle asked.

"Nah, I already ate some."

"Half the box," Terrence added.

Hannah put on an innocent expression that Michelle didn't believe for a second.

"Don't spoil your appetite," she warned.

Hannah snorted. She could out-eat a teenage boy when she felt like it.

Michelle enjoyed the movie, and pretended for a while that everything was fine. Ignoring the transformation and her worries for her family. But as she and Terrence got ready for bed, words that needed to be spoken hovered in her brain.

"I love you," she said as he got into bed beside her.

He brushed a hand over her hair. "I love you, too."

"Mom told me that love was dangerous. It would only hurt, and wasn't worth it. But she was wrong. I've loved you since the day I met you, and I swear I will never forget you, even after a thousand years." Her voice shook, but her words stayed strong.

"I love you forever," he said, fixing his eyes on hers. "And who knows? Maybe we'll see each other again. You can take me throughout space, going from star to star."

She laughed. "You and Hannah come up with the craziest things."

Michelle hesitated. "If I don't get to tell you ..." Her words wouldn't come out.

"No goodbyes," he said firmly. "Not for us. Deal?"

"Deal."

Michelle woke up one morning to agony. Every fiber of her being screamed in pain. She wondered if this was what humans felt when they burned from fire. She moaned through dry, cracked lips that wouldn't be soothed by any balm or medicine.

"Hurts," she mumbled.

Terrence woke up, rolled over, and swore. "Babe, try and drink some water."

He held a bottle to her lips. The water sizzled when it touched her skin.

"Need outside," Michelle gasped. It was time. She had to be outside, or Terrence would die in the blaze.

Terrence touched her arm, and hissed in pain. He jerked his hand away. Blisters started to form on the calloused skin. Michelle stared in horror. She'd hurt him.

She'd hurt Terrence.

"Hannah!" Terrence bellowed. "Get in here! Hurry!"

Hannah banged the door open and rushed to her mother's side. "Dad, get away!"

He jumped out of the bed just as flames sprang from Michelle's skin. Hannah grabbed her mother's arm, suppressing the flames with her own magic.

"We can't take the car, we'll have to run," Hannah snapped, taking charge effortlessly.

She hoisted Michelle in a fireman's carry and ran for the stairs. The extra weight didn't faze her at all. Terrence ran past them in the hallway, opening the front door so Hannah didn't have to slow down. Barely conscious, Michelle fought the flames burning under her skin, demanding release. Terrence was too close. She'd kill him if she transformed now.

Hannah ran towards the large hill just outside their yard. They'd cleared it of any trees. The grass would catch fire, but Hannah was strong enough to suppress it. Terrence started to follow them up the hill, but Hannah warned him off.

Hannah set her mother down gently on the grass. Embers sparked on Michelle's skin as she lay on the ground. Her head lolled back. She couldn't speak, couldn't think. She wanted to say goodbye. Burning light blinded her, obscuring her daughter's face.

"I love you," Hannah whispered. "Goodbye."

The pain vanished. Flesh became fire, and the phoenix shot into the sky.

"I love you!" Her husband's shout followed her into the atmosphere.

The phoenix soared higher, away from the ground, away from the air itself. Clouds thinned and disappeared. The heavy pressure of the air ceased. She raced through the void of space, directly towards the flaming sun that beckoned her, the irresistible call of home. Her kin streaked from the surface to meet her with flares of heat and light, singing for joy, shouting greetings.

The phoenix was home.

The Mystery

Janeen Ippolito

death came
with a curse and a charm
one for the proud
one for the vain
and a third consolation
for those without artifice
on their knees
"for you
for your woe
for your awe
for your guilt
for your weakness
for you"
for them
death came
with a grace
a mystery
of hope

About the Authors

Sophia Heotzler graduated from Geneva College with a BA in English literature. She grew up with deaf parents, making her first language American Sign Language. She loves to pour this unique perspective in her writing by using visual language to explore inner conflict and relational challenges. Inspired by authors like Jane Austen, C.S. Lewis, and J.K. Rowling, Sophia loves to blend real life issues with fantastic imagery.

Rosalie Valentine is a storyteller and lover of Jesus. When she isn't blogging, reading, or rearranging her coffee mug collection, you can probably find her writing about characters in fantasy worlds or distant galaxies. Her first collection of short stories, *Stars and Soul*, released in 2018 with praise from Nadine Brandes and New York Times bestselling author Tosca Lee.

C.W. Briar is the author of the dark fantasy novel *Whispers From The Depths*. He also has a number of short stories published in various anthologies. He lives in Upstate New York with his family and their corgi pack.

Savannah Grace is a Nebraskan author who loves writing—and reading—a good speculative story, because there's no better place to escape than in a book. When not lost in other worlds, Savannah can be found laughing way too loudly, chatting with her friends, or eating as much Korean food as she can get her hands on. She is an editor for Havok Publishing, has had her fiction pieces published in various places, and can be found at savannahgracewrites.blogspot.com or on Instagram (@savannahgraceauthor).

Beka Gremikova lives, writes, and dreams from the Ottawa Valley, Ontario, Canada. When she's not globe-trotting, searching for Narnia, or exploring new cultures, she's gushing over anime and manga, BBC classical adaptations, and video game characters.

"Nothing More Than Death," her fantasy debut in the *A Kind of Death* anthology, is dedicated to the memory of her beloved mother Heather, who passed away in November 2018 after a brave fight against cancer.

Kristina Mahr devotes her days to numbers and her nights to words. She works full-time as an accountant in the suburbs of Chicago, but her true passion is writing. In her spare time, she enjoys spending time with her family, friends, and small herd of rescue animals, as well as waking up at the crack of dawn every weekend to watch the Premier League.

Anna Tan grew up in Malaysia, the country that is not Singapore. She is the author of two fantasy books, *Coexist* and *Dongeng*, has short stories included in various anthologies and is the editor of *NutMag*, an annual zine published by MYWriters Penang. As a recipient of the Chevening Scholarship 2018/2019, Anna is currently completing an MA in Creative Writing: The Novel at Brunel University London. Anna is interested in Malay/Nusantara and Chinese legends and folklore in exploring the intersection of language, culture, and faith.

H. A. Titus can usually be found with her nose in a book or spinning storyworlds in her head. She loves mythology, RPGs, and a good cup of coffee or tea. She lives in Missouri with her weather-mage husband and two super-villain sons (don't mind the robotic dinosaurs, they're friendly) who enjoy dragging her into real-life adventures. Some claim she is half-fae, but that's just unfounded rumor.

Savannah Jezowski is the author of *The Neverway Chronicles*, *When Ravens Fall*, and *The Whitby Tales*. She specializes in gritty worlds, strong characters, and bursts of frolicking humor. When she isn't writing, she likes to watch *Castle*, *Doctor Who*, *Fringe*, and all the *Star Trek*, *Star Wars*, and BBC period miniseries she can find. She also likes to spend her days canning veggies from her garden, goofing off with her family, and working on sparkly cover designs.

Zimri A. Z. Zoran is a Tea Drinker, Cat Collector, Introvert bordering on absolute hermitude. When he's not partaking in the standard authorial clichés, he's drowning his stories in sarcastic satire and metaphor with a healthy serving of adventure and sometimes a dash of romance. Still a stranger to the world of published work, he's currently scheming his inevitable conquest.

Bethany A. Jennings is a YA fantasy author, sandwich aficionado, and star-loving night owl. In addition to her work as acquisitions editor at Uncommon Universes Press, she is a freelance editor and graphic designer, and also runs #WIPjoy, a popular hashtag game for authors. Born in SoCal, Bethany now lives in New England with her husband, four kids, zero pets, and a large and growing collection of imaginary friends.

Katherine Massengill began making up stories at the age of six, and started writing them down in high school. She loves reading and writing fantasy, and still checks closets for doorways to Narnia.

Janeen Ippolito believes you should own your unique words! She writes steampunk fantasy and urban fantasy, and creates writing resources, including the reference book *World Building From the Inside Out* and the creative writing guide *Irresistible World Building For Unforgettable Stories*. She's an experienced teacher, editor, author coach, and book marketing strategist. She's also the cohost of the podcast Indie Book Magic. In her spare time, Janeen enjoys sword-fighting, reading, pyrography, and eating brownie batter. Two of her goals are eating fried tarantulas and traveling to Antarctica.

CPSIA information can be obtained
at www.ICGtesting.com
Printed in the USA
BVHW071735060821
613315BV00001B/67